GOOD WITCH, BAD WITCH

AN ARIEL KIMBER HALLOWEEN SHORT STORY

MARY MARTEL

To Allison ♥
Be A Good
Witch But A Bad
Bitch.
XO
Mary Martel

OTHER WORKS BY MARY MARTEL:

The Dollhouse series:
No Mercy
Lost Faith
Dark Beginnings
Broken Pieces
Last Sins
Willow

Mercy Motorcycle Series:
Pretty Ugly
Pretty Complicated (A short Story)
Pretty Painful (Coming Soon)

Two Princes:
My King
My Queen (Coming Soon)

Ariel Kimber:
Brothers of the Flame

Love Potion

Blood Magic

The Ties that Bind

Tyson (Novella)

Good Witch, Bad Witch (Short Story)

1st Edition Published: October 2018

Cover Design by: Mary Martel

Created with Vellum

1

ARIEL

The doorbell rang and I jumped down from my spot on the kitchen counter and raced for the front door. If one of those jerks beat me to the door again then I was going to murder their asses.

Both Damien and Rain laughed at me as I raced out of the kitchen. They could laugh at me all they wanted, I couldn't help that I was super excited. It was Halloween and not only had I never gone trick or treating but I'd never passed out candy before either.

After hearing this, what he'd called "horrifying but not surprising news" Uncle Quinton had tried to force me to go trick or treating with him. We'd argued, me saying I was way too old to go and he'd claimed you were never too old for such a thing, even though he'd had no intention of going himself until he thought to force me to go. Thankfully, it was an argument I had won but, because he was Quinton, he couldn't leave it alone.

On my dresser in my bedroom at Dash's cottage, I now had twelve different bags of candy. It was outrageous and would likely take me twenty-five years to eat it all on my own and I'd get sick just trying. I'd rolled my eyes and grumbled when he'd given it to me but he hadn't cared in the least.

That was Quinton. He did what he wanted and you either got with the program (his program, of course) or you... I shook my head as I made it to the door. That was really the only option. Sometimes I won against him, but I was always the only one who ever did. And I think he let me win sometimes because I was the girl in the group. The only girl.

No pressure, though, right?

Puh-*lease.*

I pulled the door open after unlocking it and couldn't keep the grin off of my face when I looked down at the small children standing on the stoop before me. An angel, a black kitty cat, a Transformer and a Ninja Turtle stood there with serious looks on their faces and open bags and buckets held up and waiting.

"Trick or treat," they shouted at me in unison and my grin turned into an out and out smile. They were too cute to be true.

"You're a witch!" The little kitty cat shouted gleefully at me.

I grabbed the the bucket full of candy off of the floor and pushed open the heavy screen door. I held the bucket down in front of them and shook it wildly at them.

I didn't comment when they each grabbed a handful of candy out of the bucket as opposed to one piece each. This was my first year and I planned on doing things the right way. One rinky dink piece of candy per kid was not going to fly with me.

"I like your hat," the Ninja Turtle yelled at me.

"Thanks," I muttered happily.

There was a reason to like my hat because it was freaking awesome. It was a tall, black, pointy tipped witches' hat that wasn't cheap *or* flimsy in any way. And, no matter how I moved or what I was doing, it stood up straight and proud and never wilted. Though, if I ran it would sometimes fly off.

Quinton had picked out my outfit for me when I'd refused to get a costume for myself. The black, form fitting up top but flowing skirt on bottom, dress he'd given me screamed vintage and was not brand new when he'd given it to me. That was, I suspected, because it had been worn by some long since dead actual witch at some point in time. I figured he'd dug it out of that mysterious storage facility he had somewhere that'd I'd only heard about but had never been given the chance to visit. But I had some fancy, old school furniture that looked to be expensive that had come from there. And now a kick ass dress that screamed *witch.*

He'd even enlisted Damien in his mission and I now had fantastic black, pointed toe, lace up the front ankle boots that weren't exactly comfortable but looked fabulous on my feet. I'd likely never wear them again, but they'd go on the floor in my coffin closet with the rest of my new, fabulous boots.

The adorable children took their now heavier bags of candy and ran down the cement pathway to the front sidewalk where two bored looking teens waited for them. I imagined them to be older siblings who'd been saddled with the younger kids on a night where they'd rather be off partying it up with their friends but their parents had had better ideas.

I let the screen door slam shut as I closed the front door and twisted the lock on the doorknob. Locking the doors was a rule we all had to live by now, the guys were too paranoid to have it any other way. Too much had happened, and none of it had been good.

I didn't mind, I felt safer with the door being locked, even when I was in a house full of guys who could wield magic like a weapon and had no problem defending not only themselves but me as well. I was safest with them, but precautions always had to be taken.

"You let them take too much candy," Dash grumbled from

the living room and I immediately backtracked, heading towards the tiny living room instead of the even tinier kitchen.

"I know," I cheerfully agreed with him as I plopped down onto the sofa beside him.

Dash's lips curled up in the ghost of a smile as I leaned into him. He lifted his arm and wrapped it around my shoulders, holding me close. I looked up at him and couldn't keep the happy, loopy look off of my face.

His eyes dropped to my mouth and a fire lit inside them before they came back up to my eyes. The ghost was gone almost as if it hadn't been there in the first place and I wasn't surprised to see it gone. Dash didn't smile much and only did so when he was interacting with me. He saved his smiles for me because nothing else gave him a reason to be happy.

Dash was the only redhead in our group and he was pale with skin covered in lovely freckles. He was also a broody bastard, my roommate and one of my seven boyfriends.

Yes, I said *seven.*

It was outrageous even to me. But it was my coven, and that's the way of the witch world I'd recently been introduced into. It wouldn't have mattered to me either way because there was no choosing just one of them for me, not ever. It was an all or nothing deal I'd been resigned to at first but had since fully embraced.

"How much candy do you have left?" He asked me quietly.

About seven thousand more pounds, I wanted to tell him but didn't. If I bitched then Quinton would magically appear and give me grief for it when I was supposed to be having a good time, and bitching apparently did not go hand in hand with having a good time. I would know, he'd told me so himself at least three different times in the last twenty-four hours.

Instead, I hedged, "There's more than enough candy left to pass out."

"Are you sure the twins haven't gotten into it?" He asked as he lifted a strand of my ash blonde hair and twirled it around his finger.

I nodded even though I actually wasn't sure. I would be sure now to try and get them to eat most of my candy when they came over, that way I could push it off on Quinton as having eaten it myself and no one would be the wiser.

That sounded like an excellent plan to me.

Dash's lips twitched and I had the uncomfortable suspicion that he knew I'd been lying and he was amused by it. Amused by me.

I'd let that go. For now.

"What are you doing here?" I asked him curiously.

I hadn't expected all of them to show up at Damien and Julian's tiny house and, until they had all showed up, I hadn't even known everyone would fit in here.

He arched an eyebrow. Not arrogantly, but because he thought I should have known the answer to that question already and shouldn't have wasted breath asking.

"Yeah, yeah," I grumbled. "I'm here so you're here. I've heard this one before."

I rolled my eyes. That was what the guys always said. If I was there, then that's where they wanted to be. I hadn't thought to include Dash in this because we lived together and he spent the most amount of time with me.

"I like candy," Dash said, lying to me.

I wanted to roll my eyes at him a-*freaking*-gain but refrained from doing so. Again, we lived together, he wasn't fooling me.

"You don't eat candy," I argued with him.

His lips tipped up a little bit further and he was incredibly close to an actual smile taking over his face.

"Quinton." He said the name as if it were the only answer I

needed and in a way he was not wrong. Command performance, Uncle Quint had seen to it.

This did not make me feel good.

"You don't have to stay," I told him quietly as I laid my head down on his shoulder. "I'll tell Quinton to get over himself and he won't say anything to you. Promise."

That last part was a bold faced lie and we both knew it. Quinton would do whatever the hell he wanted and that would simply be that.

"I'm staying," Dash murmured quietly as he pressed the side of his head into the top of mine and let go of my hair.

"But-" I tried to protest but he stopped me.

"I think you forget sometimes," he muttered. "My childhood wasn't any better than your own and I've never had a Halloween before, either."

My heart stuttered in my chest and I immediately felt ashamed. Not everything was always about me and I couldn't even believe I had forgotten about Dash's childhood. He wore the marks of the abuse he'd suffered in his childhood all over his body but, what was more, they were in his eyes for all to see.

I was so stupid for not thinking about anyone besides myself. Hadn't I just promised one of the guys that I wouldn't be selfish anymore and I would focus on more than my own needs, more than my own wants and feelings? Yeah, I had. And now I was dropping the ball on that shit and that certainly didn't feel good either.

"I'm sorry," I whispered and I wanted to kick myself in the ass.

He applied pressure to my shoulders, squeezing, not painfully, but to get my attention. He didn't need to squeeze, he already had my full attention. He always did.

"Don't apologize to me," he whispered fiercely. "I fucking love that you forget. That you don't see those horrible things that happened to me during my childhood when you look at me. I've never had that with a female before because I've never had anything other than a physical relationship with a female before you."

I sighed heavily and wished like hell I had never brought this subject up for him. I had my own physical scars and I really did not like it when people touched them or pointed them out to me. The most prominent one was on my face, so it was kind of hard for me to cover up and hide from the world. The rest were on my collar bones and upper shoulders so they were easy enough to hide. Dash, on the other hand.... well... his weren't so easy to hide. If he took off his shirt and you got a look at his back or his stomach then you got a good look at his scars. His entire back was covered in layer upon layer of scar tissue and his stomach showcased the stab wounds he'd received right before I had received the wicked scar on my face that was now white and not an angry red. All thanks to Jules and his affinity for healing magic. Dash hadn't let Jules work his magic on him and had instead decided to showcase his scars because he didn't like to be touched by most people, even his brothers.

The whole thing made me sad and wished I had never opened my big, stupid mouth.

"Dash," I croaked out.

"Don't," he whispered fiercely as he pressed two fingers to my lips, stopping me from speaking. My lips closed and I swallowed thickly.

Shit.

We lived together. Yeah, we didn't share the same bedroom, we each had our own, but I used to sleep in his bed until I didn't sleep good at all and had troubles. Then, we moved to sleeping in my bed underneath the lovely yellow and black dreamcatcher Tyson had made for me that held enough of his magic and blood to keep the bad out while I slept peacefully and couldn't be touched by the bad. Even though the rest of the guys claimed Dash could sleep like the dead, he always woke up when I had trouble sleeping or was chased down by bad dreams. My bad dreams never sat well with him and he'd insisted on us sleeping in my bed together, under my dreamcatcher.

Needless to say, living together and sleeping in the same bed together, I had seen my fair share of his scars and he'd seen all of mine. I didn't know why, but it killed me to hear him talk about himself like that because I didn't see his scars when I looked at him, I just saw him. The scars were only a small part of all the beauty that was Dash. He'd earned those scars, just like I had mine, and we were two peas in one fucked-up, messed-up, abused pod.

But, we were together. That was what was important. And I didn't understand why in the hell we were talking about this.

Tonight was supposed to be fun. A new experience. Something to be happy about.

If Uncle Quint walked in on us like this... he'd kick Dash's ass for making me look so sad when he'd gone to so many lengths to make me happy. I didn't want him to see me like this because it had only just occurred to me that I wasn't the only one he'd wanted to experience this particular brand of happy. It wasn't just for me, or about me, that Quinton had pushed so hard to make this night happen.

I hadn't realized until then that there were others in our group who might not have experienced things like Halloween like a normal adolescent because of the way they'd been raised and the fact they'd been kept away from normal, non-magical children.

In order to save the rest of the night and not drag this down any further, I needed to get off the subject and turn things around to something better, happier.

"So, uhh," I drawled, "why didn't he make you dress up for

tonight like he made me do? I've been wearing this get up all damn day. And not because I wanted to. He forced this on me against my will. I swear, Dash, if I'd straight up refused to wear this dress he would have held me down and dressed me in it himself in order to get what he wanted. Or, maybe it's better described as in order to get what he thought I really wanted even though I was vehemently against it. He's crazy, Dash, and I think he gets crazier by the day. I mean, Christmas is coming up. Should I be scared?"

He chuckled and I couldn't keep the small smile off of my face at hearing it.

"We don't usually do anything for Christmas," he shared with me.

I sighed and my body relaxed in relief. "Thank goodness," I said with feeling and I meant it. I hadn't even thought about Christmas and what they did for it before just now. Honestly, I hadn't really thought much about what the future held for me outside of being here with my coven. Vivian The Imposter had never done anything for me for Christmas. She never bought me gifts, never put up a Christmas tree with bright lights and pretty ornaments. There was no fancy dinner with ham and pie and cookies and milk left out the night before for the nonexistent Santa Claus and his red nosed reindeer.

Then again, I didn't buy her gifts, either. But only because I never had any money to do so. If I'd had the money, because I was just the kind of person I was, I would have gotten her something nice every year because I'd thought she was my mother and I had loved her despite her behavior towards me.

"You okay, honey?" He asked me quietly.

Damn.

I was supposed to be changing the subject here for the better, not the worst. I had failed spectacularly because I'd gone and made myself sad and that was the exact opposite of where I needed to be. And, if I was sad he wasn't going to be happy. Also, if Quinton saw me like this he'd lose his mind and probably force feed me miniature candy bars in an attempt to make me enjoy every second of Halloween. It probably wouldn't hurt that it would go a long way towards fattening me up and they were constantly harping on me and riding my ass about eating because they wanted me to gain weight. They weren't nasty or mean about it, they just wanted me to be healthy, to look healthy, and they weren't wrong to be concerned about me in that department. A lifetime of living off of Ramen noodles and Saltine crackers hadn't really put a lot of meat on my bones and food wasn't always my first priority

I cleared my throat and hoped like hell I could clear my thoughts away as easily as I had my throat.

It was never that easy, though.

"Yeah," I muttered. "I'm fine." Then, so he wouldn't think I was lying to him, I continued to share, "I was just remembering Christmas time with Vivian and how not special it was. We never celebrated or did anything for it. There was never any gifts or stockings filled with goodness. Sometimes, if she'd get a holiday bonus at work, she'd get herself a little something special and call it her gift to herself. It was usually some expensive pair of shoes or a slutty dress. Something that would rope in another man for her in hopes of him maybe one day being the person who bought her expensive shoes and more slutty, slinky, barely there dresses. And, when she did have a boyfriend, they'd always get her gifts, but it was never what she expected to get or wanted. They were always cheap. Like, a bottle of vodka they expected her to share with them so they could drink it, get loose and then have loud, disgusting sex. Or, one year, a huge turkey they expected her to cook for them. That hadn't gone over well and she'd kept the turkey but booted that guy out on his ass.

After, of course, he smacked her around for throwing his "gift" back in his face."

"You never had gifts?" He asked me in a sad voice.

I shook my head and answered honestly, "Nope."

I wasn't even sad about it, really. It had simply been the hand I had been dealt in life and, honestly, it had seemed normal to me. Until I witnessed other people bragging about what they'd been given by their parents at school after the holiday break. Then, I'd just put my head down and tried to not listen.

"Me neither," he whispered and my head jerked to the side like I'd been slapped.

I was so stupid. So goddamned stupid.

If he never did anything for Halloween of course he didn't get to do anything for Christmas. Good fucking god, what the hell was the matter with me? His mother and grandmother were arguably worse than my fake mother had been. And Dash had suffered greatly.

"Dash," I said quietly, having no words for my own insensitivity and stupidity.

"That fucking *does it,"* Quinton growled menacingly from behind the couch. I jumped guiltily and Dash flinched.

Dash pulled his arm away from my shoulders and stood up abruptly. He whirled around to glare at Quinton. I scrambled, turning around and placed my knees into the couch. I leaned against the couch and propped my elbows up on the back of it.

I wasn't surprised in the slightest to see him standing there.

He ignored Dash and glared at me angrily.

"Where in the fuck is your hat?" He growled at me.

My eyebrows shot up in confusion and I raised my hand and patted the top of my head only to find the damn hat in question missing.

"Huh," I muttered to myself under my breath. "It was there when I answered the door for the trick or treaters that last time.

It must have fallen off sometime between me locking the door and sitting down here on the couch."

I lowered my hands and put my elbows back into the couch. I screwed up my nose and stuck my tongue out at Quinton. He sighed heavily, his shoulders drooped and he leaned his back against the wall in defeat.

"How long have you been standing there listening to us talk?" Dash asked in a low, dangerous voice.

Damn.

I chewed on my lip ring in a nervous habit and, if I'd been wearing shorts or leggings, I would have rubbed my suddenly sweaty palms against my thighs. I couldn't do that with this outrageous, yet very fabulous, dress that I'd been forced to wear because I didn't want to leave any marks on it or mess it up in any way. I had no idea how to clean a dress like this that was as old as dirt. With my luck, I'd put it in the washer and the damn thing would either eat it or it'd come out covered in bleach spots even if I hadn't put bleach in there with it.

It was outrageous, but I had that kind of bad luck. Sometimes it sucked to be me. Other times, especially lately, it was freaking awesome to be me.

Quinton tore his eyes off of me and turned his angry glare on Dash.

"Not long, but long enough," he said casually. "It also doesn't hurt that your voice can never be too quiet in this shitty little house. Everybody can hear you even when they're all the way on the other side of the house and all the doors in-between are closed."

This, sadly, was the truth. Though, I didn't think it was a shitty little house. Little, yes. Shitty, no. I didn't think it was worth arguing with Quinton over, unless Damien or Julian came in here and were offended by his harsh words because he was right and wherever they were in the house, they'd most likely heard what he'd had to say.

"God damn it," Dash muttered angrily and I winced. Unless he was being an asshole, which he hadn't been towards me since our first meeting, he was always a very calm, rational person who never so much as raised his voice at anyone. I think it was because it took too much effort for him to get angry and he wasn't about to waste his time when he knew just how precious his time and energy were.

Hearing the anger in his voice now was a surprise to me. I hadn't thought anything we were saying was a secret and I certainly wouldn't have said it in a house full of other people if I hadn't been okay with other people hearing about it in the first place.

"It's not a big deal and we're all going to forget about it," I said confidently.

"Fine," Quinton grunted, knowing exactly what I was doing. "But, I just want you to know that you should probably brace for Christmas because we are going to celebrate this year and no amount of bitching on your part is going to get either of you out of it."

My eyes widened in surprise and I opened my mouth to demand he take it back immediately. I didn't want him changing their lives because of me. That was absurd.

"No," he barked at me. "I'm not going to stand here and listen to any of your bullshit. Not today. Not ever. And, baby, you're going to suck it up and give this to me because it's what I need you to do for me, it's what I need you to give me. For my sake and peace of mind, I need to give you the things you've never had before."

He uncrossed his arms to raise a fist and thumped it against his chest, over his heart and my breath caught in my throat as my chest tightened at witnessing this action.

"It makes me happy and I need it," he whispered fiercely as his eyes shone brightly while he stared me down.

I didn't like the bright in his eyes or the raw emotion in his voice. I'd done that to him, I'd put that emotion there, and I didn't like knowing I was to blame at all.

So, I did the only thing I could think of to make the situation better. I gave him what he wanted.

"Okay," I told him in a quiet, sweet voice. "If that's what you want, then that's what you're going to get."

Oh, shit. I couldn't believe I'd just said that. I'd given it all away and, with that one sentence, I'd made my feelings for him blatantly obvious for anyone who'd been paying attention and knew me well enough to take notice.

I loved him. And I was terrified of him finding out about it.

His face immediately softened and I fought the urge to backpedal and do or say something to take the words and their meaning back.

"Shit," Dash swore under his breath and I felt a full-blown panic attack coming my way. He'd heard the meaning behind my voice and, like Quinton, he'd understood the feelings behind them.

Shit was right. This was not good for me at all.

My chest rose and fell heavily with each hurried breath I took. If I passed out because I couldn't get in enough air because I was on the verge of a panic attack because I was afraid Quinton finally figured out that I loved him, then I would never live it down and I'd be so embarrassed and mortified with myself.

To do it in front of Dash would make it all the worse and I'd never be able to look him in the eye again without my face flaming bright red.

Quinton stood up straight and came at me, fast. Before I had time to blink he held my face in his hands and was inches away from me, his face hovering in front of mine.

"Breathe, baby," he whispered. "Take a deep breath and try and calm down for me. It's all gonna be good, I promise."

I believed him. If I could only do what he said, then it would certainly be all good.

I sucked in a sharp breath and slowly released it, immediately calming down while I stared into Quinton's dark, bottomless eyes.

Heat poured into me through his hands on my face and I was just suddenly calm and once again in control of my raging emotions and run-away heart.

"What did you do to me?" I asked in a hoarse whisper.

I didn't actually think he'd done anything to me, but it was the only logical explanation for the sudden change that'd come over me.

"It's not anything I did to you," he whispered back in a strong, confident voice. "It's all about who you are to me and who I am to you."

I didn't want to ask because I was terrified of the answer I was almost certain he'd give to me.

Because I was stupid and could never help myself, I asked anyway.

"And what is that you think I am to you and what is that you think you are to me?" I asked.

"I'm yours," he whispered smugly and the light in his eyes brightened with each word. "And you're mine."

Yeah.

That was what I was afraid of him saying.

2

QUINTON ALEXANDER

Christ.

Jesus fucking Christ.

I knew she felt deep for me, I didn't think she was capable of not going in deep when it came to the people she cared about and it scared the shit out of me for her. But, I had no fucking idea she'd felt *that* deep and at that level for me.

If I was a hopeful man I'd almost think she loved me.

I wasn't that kind of man, though. I didn't get hopeful and I didn't wish for things. If I wanted something for myself or my family, then I went out and put in the work and the effort to make it happen so I could get what I wanted.

That's what I had planned on doing with Ariel and would continue to do, despite the fact she'd just given me what she'd given me. I was going to put in the work and earn it from her like I did everything else. And I was going to work my ass off for it, I'd do next to anything for her and to earn her love.

That look in her eyes just now when she'd so easily given me exactly what I wanted despite it not being what she wanted in the slightest? Yeah, I caught that look. And it almost fucking unmanned me seeing it coming off of her.

That look screamed she felt deep for me and maybe even loved me. I wasn't sure I'd earned that level of emotions from her yet, but I was a selfish bastard and I'd take whatever I could get from her. I'd also be waiting for her to give me the words because I wanted to hear them come out of her mouth almost more than I wanted my next breath so I could live.

She was fucking everything to me and she was fucking everything to my brothers.

I dropped my hands from her overheated face, something I knew I was to blame for, and bent forward to kiss her forehead. I wanted to put my mouth on hers but wasn't going to push it with her with Dash being in the room. I didn't think either of them were ready for that kind of PDA.

Dash used to sleep around with any piece of ass he could get his hands on and he switched up girls monthly. Of course, that all stopped the moment Ariel walked into our lives. But, post Ariel, even though we'd known about all of the action he'd gotten, we'd never heard word one about it out of his mouth. If we heard about it it was because we'd gone into town and were at the bar or the grocery store or the fucking gas station, and some dumb broad was talking about him with her friends or it was a friend who'd heard about him and all the girls he'd blown through. They've been gossiping about him in town since he discovered pussy and what he could do with it. But never, not fucking ever, did he talk about it or the girls he'd fucked around with. He wasn't that kind of guy and we only knew about it because he couldn't hide shit from us when there were so many of us and we all had keys to everyone's houses, not that the fucker had locked his doors before our girl had moved in with him. So, with any of us showing up out there at his cottage whenever the mood struck us to visit, it was kind of hard for him to hide some chick that he had over and was doing.

We'd seen a lot of them come and go and none of them ever

stuck around longer than a month save for the last one, and I think she only stuck that long because we'd gone camping over the summer and he hadn't actually had to be around her or have anything to do with her for the entire duration of our camping trip. We got home, introduced ourselves to Ariel, and the bitch was gone the very next day.

Now Ariel lived with him and they were tight. I didn't think it was because they lived together that they were so close because I think she'd started off not liking anything about him outside of his stupid, fleabag, asshole of a cat. She'd overheard something unpleasant he'd said in regards to her and hadn't wanted to like him afterwards. But he'd liked her and I don't think him turning into a nice guy was what won her over, either.

I don't think she really liked him until they'd gone through something horrible and incredibly traumatic happening to the two of them at the same time. They'd bonded over shared blood and pain and I no longer questioned her feelings for him or his for her. They were solid and that relationship had a foundation that could not be cracked under any kind of weight or pressure.

But, because Dash was Dash, I didn't think he'd enjoy watching me make out with our girl in front of him since he was such a private person when it came to intimate acts. Eventually, we'd have to talk about this and he'd have to get over himself and his hang ups because there were too many of us for each and every one of us to be watching our steps around the others and no one wanted to hide their relationship from their family. I would only hold myself back for so long before I was just done with it and was going to claim my girl whenever the fuck I wanted to. And he'd either be cool with it or have to hide the fact that he wasn't from the rest of us because I knew I wasn't the only one who didn't want to keep themselves in check when it came to our girl just because we were around the others.

I stood up straight, lifted my eyes, and stared directly at my long time brother and friend without backing down or blinking.

He dipped his head slightly in acknowledgement. He got me and he knew exactly what I was saying. I sighed in relief. The last thing I wanted was to make anyone uncomfortable so that I myself wouldn't have to feel something unfortunate that I didn't want to. It would have put me in a horrible position and I would have felt awful about it. I wouldn't have stopped what I was doing because I didn't think that was any way to live my life, but I'd feel bad doing it and it would sting and take just a little bit of the joy out of it.

He didn't need to say it, it was blatantly obvious. He loved her too. Loved her so much that his feelings for her likely rivaled my own. He was like Ariel, like me, and he too felt deep. We didn't do shit in halves or by small measures.

"I'm buying you a Christmas present," I told him smugly.

He shook his head and muttered, "Don't expect me to return the favor, Quint. You'll be in for a whole world of disappointment if you expect me to go out and buy you shit for a holiday neither of us believes in and you're just doing it for Ariel."

My lips twitched in amusement. I didn't honestly expect any of them to buy me shit for Christmas.

Ariel clapped her hands in glee as her torso swiveled around and the upper half of her body faced Dash.

"Oh my gosh," she breathed out in an excited rush. "Presents! I get to buy everyone presents. I've never bought someone a present before. Dash! This is the perfect time to get you something. It's Halloween and stores will have everything you love right now, even if it is creepy."

My lips moved up further in a half smile. She was just too damn cute sometimes.

The doorbell rang. Ariel squealed loudly and incredibly girly and my mouth dropped open at hearing the sound of it. I had never heard her make such a happy, carefree, joyous noise before and I was astonished to hear it now.

She sprang to her feet and raced out of the living room, headed in the direction of the front door.

I chuckled softly to myself at her enthusiasm to hand out candy to greedy little beggar children. It certainly wasn't my idea of a good time but she seemed to get off on it. I was glad I had forced this shit on her because she was having the time of her life tonight wearing one of my long since dead ancestors' old dresses and giving away free candy. Every time that goddamn doorbell rang her running footsteps could be heard throughout the entire house. She was loving every fucking second of this shit.

The twins were loving it too. They kept trying to beat her to the door but had stopped when they'd seen her face fall one too many times when they'd made it to the door before she had and handed out her fucking candy. It made me want to knock their heads together for robbing her of what was giving her so much joy. Until I realized why they were doing it. Once I realized why, I almost pulled Ariel aside and told her what was up, but I didn't because I didn't want to put a dark cloud over her day when she was supposed to be having a good time and experiencing new things. It hadn't occurred to me that she wasn't the only one who'd never experienced Halloween on this level before. The twins, much like every single one of us, had never gone trick or treating before or even handed out candy to little beggar children before. It was a new experience for all of us.

I, along with several of my brothers, had no desire to put on ridiculous costumes, paint our faces or whatever the fuck it was people did on this holiday, and hand out candy to kids who, in all likeliness, did not need any more sugar in their diets. If Julian hadn't told me it would have made me one serious dick, I would have filled Ariel's bucket with apples and oranges and had her hand those out to the little beggars instead of candy. Julian had been against this and had informed me I would be akin to the devil if I gave children fruit instead of candy, and he'd pointed out that it would be Ariel they would be looking at like she was evil and not me because it was her who was supposed to hand the shit out and not me. That was all it had taken to sell me on buying sugar coated shit for children.

That and I thought there might be a distinct possibility that if they got too pissed about their fruit then this might be a horribly bad thing because apples and oranges made good objects for throwing and both would hurt to get pelted with and could break windows and cause other potential damage to Julian's and Damien's shitty little house. I could do without the headache that would cause me and the going to jail part that would happen if someone threw something at my girl, whether it could hurt her or not, if someone threw something at Ariel I was going to put my fist in their face. Repeatedly. And the norms were known for calling the cops when they couldn't handle their own business. Also, it would probably be bad for my soul to beat up on children.

A presence at my back made me turn around to see Rain standing in the middle of the hallway, directly behind me and staring at his daughter standing in the open doorway. He had a rare smile on his usually cold face as he watched her. Usually, the motherfucker was as cold as ice, unless it involved his daughter. That was the only time he ever thawed out at all.

"Did I hear we're doing Christmas this year?" he asked in a quiet, smug voice.

From behind me, Dash snorted.

Fucking Christ.

I did not want to do Christmas with this man, or anybody.

But, for my family, I would because it was becoming clearer by the second that the majority of them had felt like they'd been missing out on things normal families had been doing together since the dawn of man.

And I'd give my family everything, always.

Yeah, fucking Christ, but we were all doing Christmas together. And, I'd smile even if I hated every fucking second of it.

3

ARIEL

Arms wrapped around my middle, and a big body burning with the most incredible heat, pressed up against my back.

Lips came to my ear.

"Make it burn, pretty girl," either Abel or Addison whispered in my ear, making me shiver.

I hadn't learned how to tell their voices apart yet and didn't think I ever would. Unless I could see them, I had no idea who was speaking to me. I had no hope of this getting better with time because if there was some small nuance in their voices that held a difference I would have heard it by then and, since I paid attention to everything they said or did, I would have noticed.

"Which one are you?" I whispered without taking my eyes off of the field in front of me. A field that left me with an extremely unsettled feeling in my gut.

What the hell?

He laughed, his body shaking with it, and the arms around my middle grew tighter. Not in restriction, but just to hold me closer.

"Guess," he breathed his command beside my ear.

I sighed, wishing he'd just tell me instead of making me play some sort of a game with him. I didn't like playing games much and I suspected I wasn't much of a fun person to be around most of the time. Yet, for some unknown reason, the twins always wanted to play with me.

They were insane.

I liked it. Most of the time.

Since I had a fifty-fifty chance of getting it right, I guessed instead of just insisting he tell me. I had a feeling he'd make me wish I had just guessed in the first place and given him what he wanted right off the bat.

I sighed, and said, "Abel." Guessing on my Pepper twin.

Addison and Abel James were identical twins all save for their eyes and hair. I'd nicknamed them the Salt and Pepper twins because Abel had jet black hair and bright, vibrant green eyes. Addison, my Salt twin, had blonde hair so light it bordered on being white and blue, summer sky eyes. Their hair color gave them their nicknames. It hadn't hurt that they were both weirdly into the colors white and black.

To my knowledge, they were blissfully unaware of my cute little nicknames for them. But, Quint knew, and I was sure he'd tell them whenever it was most convenient for him. I hoped that time came never because I had no desire to put up with the massive amount of bullshit they would give me because of it.

"Do you want it to be Abel?" He asked and something unpleasant slithered through me.

I couldn't believe that he'd ask me something like that. I had never picked between the two of them and had never even showed preference between them. To me, they were a unit. You couldn't have one without the other so I never looked at them separately.

"Why would you ask me that?" I demanded to know. His body strung tight, and I knew all traces of humor had left him.

"So, you don't want it to be Abel?" He asked stiffly.

I growled angrily under my breath. There was no winning for losing here with him. Whoever the hell he was.

I jerked away from him, wrenching myself out of his arms and spun around to face him. I came face to face with my Pepper twin. Black hair as dark as a moonless night and eyes as vibrant and green as emeralds greeted me. I had to look up to meet his green eyes because the twins were incredibly tall, so I'd had to look up, and I wasn't a short girl. They were tall and built well, with thicker bodies than any of the other guys in our group were.

I shook my head as I glared at Abel James.

"I don't have a preference between you and your brother, Abel," I gritted out harshly. "I would have thought that by now you'd know that, but it would seem I was wrong."

Being wrong didn't feel all too good. I had thought he knew me better than that and it hurt to know that he didn't.

"Everyone has a preference between the two of us," he grunted angrily. "Always has been like that, except for our parents."

I shook my head and a small, bitter laugh escaped me. What was the matter with this guy? He couldn't be serious, could he?

"This isn't funny, Ariel." He growled at me.

He was right, it wasn't funny at all. It was all kinds of sad and left me feeling incredibly unamused and I had no idea why I'd laughed in the first place.

"You're right," I repeated my thought, only part of it though. I didn't want to start some kind of stand off with him when we were supposed to be meeting the others further out in the field and a quick look that way told me they were waiting for us and who the hell knew how long they'd been there for. "None of this shit is funny at all, and it's not funny because you are being downright ridiculous and I can't even handle standing here talking to you, that's how ridiculous you're being."

He'd flinched when I'd said the word shit, and now his face looked stricken.

"Look," I huffed in frustration as I reached up and gestured to what I was wearing with my hand, running it from breast down to my knee. "I'm not exactly comfortable here wearing this getup and I'd like to get this over with so I can go back to Dash's and put some actual clothes on again. Not that I've really been wearing what I'd normally call actual clothes today, but clothes that have been straight up ridiculous all damn day long. Whatever this is that I'm being let into for the first time, I'm sure it's going to be cool because I love magic and I love all things that have to do with it, but this crap, being out here like this, it's a whole lot of *uncool* and, even though we've just started, I'm already wayyyyyyy over it."

None of this was a lie.

Somewhere between passing out candy to curling up on the couch and watching a scary movie with Damien, the rest of the guys had bailed, saying they'd had something to do and places to be, Rain included. Somewhere between there and falling asleep on said couch, the guys had decided how we'd be spending the rest of our Halloween night.

So, now we were here. And I hadn't been given much of a choice, like what had been going on for the majority of the entire day. Not that I minded, the day had actually been pretty awesome and I'd enjoyed most of it, outside of my verbally sparring with Quinton several times over.

So, now was now and if I felt uncomfortable in that ancient dress earlier because it was ancient and I didn't want to accidentally ruin it, I really had no freaking idea what uncomfortable was because now I really was *uncomfortable* on a whole new level that had probably passed uncomfortable and left it behind in the dust as soon as I'd removed my dress and slipped this getup on. Not that there had been much I'd slipped on. I'd just mostly removed clothing and had been left embarrassed by the lack of clothing I'd put back on.

Quinton had magnanimously told me I could keep my bra and panties on underneath the black, hooded robe he'd handed me after he'd ushered me up the stairs of the big house and showed me to the bedroom I'd been given there and had only used once before. He'd pulled the heavy robe out of the walk-in closet that, when I peeked inside when his back was turned, I noted had become over half way full. This was something I was choosing to ignore because if I thought about how much money and time had been wasted on clothes for me I'd likely never get the chance to wear in the next forty-eight years, I would freak out and demand they return all of it. Which, in no way, would they do. I'd shoved his ass out the door and had slammed the door to the closet shut so I wouldn't have to see the evidence of their outrageous behavior. I usually didn't have to spend time at the big house and told myself I could easily forget all about the innards of that offensive closet.

Then, I'd set about disrobing until everything had been removed save for my black, cotton, matching bra and panties. I'd gone for comfort and not something to be seen in because I'd known I'd be keeping my clothes on and, under no circumstances, would the guys or anybody else be seeing me in them.

Boy, had I been wrong about that shit.

In order to not be standing around in my underthings, I'd hurriedly put my robe on, tied the front of it shut and pulled the hood over my head. It still hadn't been enough, not by any means.

Before I'd shoved Quinton out of the bedroom, he'd shared with me we were going through the woods and out to the field he'd caught me spying on the guys before when they'd been prancing around naked under their robes, circling round and round a blazing fire pit. Their robes hadn't been enough for them at the time, either, because I'd seen more than what I should have seen and enough to make me feel like a Peeping Tom.

Now, it seemed like it'd be their turn to look their fill but only the censored version because of my prudish behavior.

They hadn't waited for me while I'd changed into my robe and I'd thought I had been left entirely alone. Until Abel had creeped up behind me, that is.

And now I was seriously uncomfortable, embarrassed, and way the hell over this shit.

When he just stood there sullenly, staring at me, I sighed heavily. This wasn't going anywhere, we weren't going anywhere, not until we'd had this uncomfortable and outrageous conversation over with.

"Abel," I growled, voice low. "They are waiting on us." I flung my hand dramatically in the direction of the guys in the field. "It's rude of us to stand here when they are all over there and waiting on us. I don't want to be rude, I want to get this *over with.*"

His eyes narrowed on me as he placed his hands on his wide hips.

I sighed again at seeing this gesture that screamed at me he wasn't about to walk away until we had this out. Whatever the hell it was.

I wanted to scream.

"I just want to know that you see me too," he murmured quietly, surprising me.

"What?" I asked incredulously, now really not believing this was happening because there was no way in this universe where either of my Salt and Pepper twins weren't confident and full of themselves in a way I'd almost found unnerving. "What the hell are you talking about? You're standing right in front of me, of course I see you."

I scoffed.

Had he been drinking or something? I hadn't been around any of the guys when they'd imbibed in alcohol, but I wasn't stupid, I knew it had to happen occasionally. It was Halloween and all, maybe he'd been partying it up and I hadn't realized it because I hadn't really been paying attention to him *or* his brother because I'd been too busy sucking in every ounce of joy I'd been able to get out of passing candy out to little people and, as the night wore on, slightly bigger people. And when I hadn't been doing that, I'd been in the pint sized living room, eyes on nothing other than whatever horror movie that'd been playing on the big screen at the time. I hadn't paid particular attention to any of the guys outside of who'd been standing or sitting beside of me at the time, and they'd only been there because they'd put themselves there, not because I had sought them out.

"That's not what I meant," he said in low voice that was full of hurt and disgust.

Shit.

This was not going good, and my being abrupt and sarcastic with him really wasn't helping out my situation any. At this rate, we'd be standing here until the rest of the guys came to investigate and I knew that if they did that then Abel would prove he was just like his brother and he'd take off on me. Unless, of course, I gave him a reason not to.

It was safe to say, I wasn't very good at this relationship thing and I was even worse when it came to talking about my feelings or other girly things and I *really* sucked at talking to other people about their emotions and feelings when it came to our relationship we shared together. I had never had a healthy example to follow by and thought that had a good deal to do with why I'd always managed to eff everything up.

"Then what *did* you mean?" I asked in exasperation, further effing this whole situation up and not even knowing how to stop myself if I wanted to try. And, I was pretty sure I wanted to try.

"I want to know that you don't see Addison when you look at me," he whispered.

I flinched.

Damn it.

This already shitty situation was getting even shittier by the second and things were really not looking good for me.

I couldn't exactly do that and be honest with him. Just like if Addison were to ask me if I saw Abel when I looked at him. I wouldn't have been able to tell him no and have it be the truth. To me, they were a cohesive unit and I would never, not ever, see one without the other. I thought that was how everyone looked at them and I'd just assumed that's how they wanted to be seen, together.

"I see you when I look at Addison," I told him quietly and honestly. "I know you're different people, it's just that... You both do almost every single thing together and you've even said things before that make me feel like it's either both of you or neither of you."

This time it was him who visibly flinched and my heart skipped a beat at seeing it.

Apparently, that had been the way wrong thing to say. Of course, me being me, I tried to make it right by blurting all of my feelings and every single thought I had running around in my crazy brain all out at once, and it really wasn't ever pretty to listen to and always embarrassing when I'd finally ceased speaking.

"Abel, please, listen to me and what it is that I'm trying to tell you," I rushed out, stumbling over my words and, even though I knew I should stop, I kept right on going all the same, like I didn't know just how stupid I sounded even though I absolutely *did.* "You and Addison are not the same person and I damn well know that. You're different people even though you both want to share everything and act certain ways that I still, to this day, do not exactly understand and often times find baffling..."

He winced and squeezed his eyes shut tightly as his hands fisted at his sides. Ignoring this, I kept right on going.

Stupidly.

"I don't see it as wrong that you two act the ways you do or think it's wrong. What I think is that it's different because you two are different. I've never met twins before meeting the two of you. And, I don't think I will ever meet another pair like either of you ever again. You guys are a unique pair and I love you both for it. But, I have to be honest with you here. At first, I'd thought the two of you were kind of odd, and then when you'd started talking about sharing everything... and when I realized you guys were talking about sharing me as well... Well, to me, who'd never even had a boyfriend before and only gone out on a handful of dates with boys that never meant anything to me and I knew they never would so I never really fully paid attention to them. But with you guys, all of you guys, I am fully invested here. Not just in the coven, which I'm never going to leave, but in this relationship that we are building between all of us. I know we-"

I stopped abruptly when he cut me off.

"It's okay, pretty girl," he muttered. "I get it. You're clearly uncomfortable and off on one of your many rambles. You can stop talking now. It's all good."

My shoulders drooped in defeat. It was clear he didn't get anything and there was absolutely nothing about this that was all good.

I just, unfortunately, didn't seem to know how to make it any better and every time I tried it just seemed to get worse and I could tell it couldn't get much worse than this. He was feeling dejected and I didn't think he cared for me all that much at the moment. I mean, I knew he cared for me, but the more I spoke, the more he looked like he was ready to get the fuck away from me and not stop until he was as far away from me as he could get without having to actually leave the state.

"I don't think-"

He cut me off again and when he did, it really pissed me off that he wasn't letting me ramble and get out what I wanted to when I wanted and how I wanted to do it.

"Like I said, it's all good, Ariel." He said and my heart squeezed inside my chest at hearing this because it was another blatant lie.

I didn't enjoy him lying to me the same way I didn't enjoy him cutting me off like that and talking over me after he refused to digest my words how I'd meant for him to take them in.

"What the hell are you two doing over here?" Addison growled darkly from behind me, and I hated that he'd been able to sneak up behind me because my back had been towards the field and the rest of the guys who were out there in it because I was turned towards the dense forest to face Abel.

I only knew it was Addison because his twin was standing right in front of me and he wasn't speaking when his twin had.

I whirled around to face my Salt twin. His body was identical to his twins. The only differences being where Abel had black hair and green eyes, Addison had white blonde hair and sky blue eyes. Other than that, they were identical. Right down to the clothes they were wearing tonight, and that being only the hooded robe I wore and it was tied tight on their chests, hiding their bodies from my view. Not that that mattered, I'd seen what they had going for them under their cloaks before in all of its male glory.

I blushed, thinking about what was hidden beneath that robe and wished like hell I hadn't been thinking about it in the first place. Just what kind of pervert was I?

"Nothing," Abel grumbled from behind me. "I was just leaving. I'll catch you at home, twin."

Oh, no he did not.

He was not going to storm off in an angry huff away from me because I was stupid enough to not check my words before I let them come out of my mouth and seemed to be an emotional moron.

I whirled back around to face Abel and pointed an angry finger in his direction, jabbing it at him.

"No," I snapped loudly. "You don't get to walk away from this. You don't get to walk away from me like this. You started this shit and you are damn well going to stick it out and finish it with me. If it were me who stormed off in an angry huff after misconstruing every single thing out of your mouth, then you'd be so pissed you would tell me, straight up, when you saw me again the next time just how big of an asshole I was for doing that. You'd also tell me it wasn't cool because, as much as you guys like to joke around and play about pretty much everything, you are still fully invested in this relationship and fully invested in me and when I'm a dick and not exactly nice or do things that are entirely selfish like leave you guys hanging in the breeze for weeks because I couldn't handle my own emotions and was acting out and like a brat... Well, you would call me out on that shit. And," I snapped my fingers at him when he opened his mouth to clearly argue with me, "don't even try to say you wouldn't because you've already called me out on my shit before, so don't even try to say otherwise."

Delicious heat hit me from behind right before an arm went around my waist and I was pulled into a body that was harder than mine and a whole lot bigger. His large hand dropped down to my hip where he gripped me tightly and pulled me even further into his side. I moved into him easily, needing the comfort.

When I was tucked in tight to Addison's side, he asked his brother, who'd been watching us with rapt attention, quietly, seriously, "What are you doing to our pretty girl, twin? Why does she seem so upset with you and why in the hell are you so ready to walk away from her, to walk away from the rest of your brothers?"

They were good questions. Questions I wouldn't have been able to think to ask myself in my current frame of mind. They were also questions that I really wanted answers to. And, not just that, but what's more, is that I wanted to know what in the heck had brought this on in the first place. I had thought we'd been in a good place, even though I knew I hadn't been able to spend as much time with them lately as I had wanted to. But I was going to try and make up for that, I'd already had plans in place to show up at the big house and steal them away to go Christmas shopping with me for the other guys. And, I'd made these plans just as soon as Quinton had brought up all of us having a big Christmas to-do together and him buying me presents. I know, I know. Damien, and by proxy, Julian, would have been the most likely choices to bring on a shopping spree with me, be it Christmas or otherwise. But I personally didn't want to go shopping with Damien. He and I were in a good place and I thought a shopping spree with him might have been just the thing to ruin that for me. My Salt and Pepper twins, though? I thought I would have a blast with them. Not to mention, I'd seen the way they had acted with the trick or treaters and how they'd rushed to beat me to the door. I didn't even think they'd been trying to beat me, but that they'd just wanted to get to the door first so they could pass out candy and take in all of the fabulous costumes that the children had shown up at the door in. Something had clicked inside me and, at the same time I had remembered all I had learned about their pasts. What I had remembered was that they'd been raised amongst their family and their parents coven. They hadn't been allowed out around the normal children or allowed to go to public school. In fact, they hadn't even been allowed to be around most other children who'd held magic or most other witches from other covens because of the way they'd looked. Because of how they looked, upon their birth, there had actually been several covens and witches who'd said they should have been killed because they claimed the twins had been born cursed.

I had never believed in things such as curses before I'd met the guys. Now, I knew different after everything I'd seen and been party to, and I absolutely knew that things like curses and people being cursed at birth were a definite possibility. Anything was possible, so I felt like there might have been a chance this was true about the twins, because, like I'd said, anything was possible. Still, I didn't think that meant you should kill your own damn children and, if they had been cursed, it was more than likely because people had been afraid of them upon their birth because of how different they were in a world where the witches and people who held magic tried to hide it from everyone around them, not wanting anyone to know what they were because they didn't want history to repeat itself. The twins stuck out like a sore thumb and would most likely always draw attention to themselves because of the way they looked when standing side by side.

Anyway, they'd been kept from other children and the lives they'd lived, so, they'd never experienced life any other way outside of the closeted one where they were hidden away from the world like treasure their parents were afraid would be stolen from them the moment someone else laid eyes on them. They, like me, had never experienced Halloween before and probably had never experienced anything of the like before. Like me. So, I had immediately decided that Christmas shopping with me was the absolute best thing that could have happened to them in the near future. They would have loved it. Right now, though, it didn't look like we'd be experiencing that any time soon.

"What the fuck have you done now?" Addison snarled at his brother as his hand bit into my hip.

Damn.

This was even worse than it had been when it had only been me and one twin. Having two of them with me right this moment was not a good thing to have at all. And this was honestly the only time I'd ever felt like I would have been better off with just having one of them on my hands.

As much as I appreciated him trying to come to my rescue, Addison didn't get to take over this conversation. I'd asked Abel what the hell he was doing and he didn't answer me. It was going to upset me even more and seriously piss me off if his twin waltzed over here, asked once, and then Abel answered him like his questions had been more important than my own.

Eyes blazing furiously, I swiveled my head around in Addison's direction. "He thinks I only see you when I look at him or something absurd like that."

Addison's lips parted and he quickly shot his brother a questioning glance.

"What?" He asked his twin incredulously.

That's what I was saying.

Abel threw up his hands in exasperation and shouted, "And I was right!"

Oh boy.

I shot a quick look over my shoulder towards the others only to see Uncle Quint heading our direction and knew I didn't have much time left to sort this shit out before he showed up and took control of the entire situation and I was worried he wouldn't make the situation any better than I'd been able to do with it.

I jerked my head back around to face forward and quickly

stepped forward moving out of Addison's arms, putting myself directly into Abel's space, not caring in the slightest that he was glaring down at me with hostility and dislike.

"Stop yelling like an asshole," I growled low at him.

"Jesus," Addison grunted from behind me and I knew I'd been swearing more than usual because they were pushing me too far and it was starting to show and I was slowly losing control over my emotions. If I didn't calm down soon my hair would probably start floating around my head. Sometimes it did that when I got too emotional and couldn't keep it under wraps.

"I told you," I snapped. "I see you two as a unit because that's what you come off as and I don't want one of you without the other one because it just wouldn't seem right to me. I don't know what the fuck your problem is but if you don't knock this crap off, you're going to cause problems for all of us and that's not cool. I told you, I see you in Addison as well. Geez, Abel, you guys are identical twins except for hair and eyes. What do you want from me and why are you doing this crap now? I don't get it."

I moved back a step and shook my head vigorously from side to side, my hair flying all around my face. I bitter laugh escaped past my lips and I couldn't stop my shoulders from drooping in defeat.

I stopped laughing and said quietly, "I don't know what you want from me."

Heat hit my back, delicious and comforting. Arms wrapped around my middle and I leaned back into Addison's big body, liking that he'd moved into me without invitation on my part. I wanted them to touch me way more than they did but didn't want to come right out and tell them that for fear of rejection. Which, before what was happening right in front of my eyes, I would have told you was a stupid waste of effort to have worried on my part. Now I was wondering if I wasn't right to worry in the first place.

"I... I..." He stammered and my heart jerked at hearing it.

"Are you possessed?" I asked him seriously.

"What?" He snapped.

What indeed.

I didn't even know if I believed in demon possession, I just knew that, from the books they'd put on my shelves, they obviously did. Which was all kinds of scary and, what was even scarier, was that Abel clearly was not acting like himself and maybe demon possession was a possibility.

Addison's cheek pressed to mine and he whispered, "He's not possessed, pretty girl. Just an asshole."

Huh.

I guess that was a relief and not one at the same time. I wasn't filled up with joy hearing the news that even Addison thought his twin was being an asshole.

"You're never around anymore," Abel spit out and my mouth dropped open.

"That's enough," Quinton growled angrily, having made it to our little huddle. "You're done here. Take your ass back to the house and I want you to stay the fuck away from her when we get back and she comes inside to put her clothes back on before going home. I want you to stay in your room until she's gone. Am I making myself clear?"

I blinked rapidly as I snapped my mouth shut and my head swiveled to the side to face Quinton. As I turned, Addison pulled his face away from mine and, without letting me go, turned to look at Quinton as well.

Did he... Did Uncle Quint just send Abel home and off to his bedroom like a naughty little child?

What, was he going to spank him next?

I turned back to Abel, ignoring Quinton and his outrageous

behavior only to see Abel had already turned around and was heading towards the house because clearly, he'd listened to Quint's words and taken them to heart and was now on his way home like the naughty child Uncle Quint had just treated him like.

Unbelievable.

"Abel," I shouted at his retreating back. "Get back here right this second."

He didn't even pause in his stride or turn back to look at me.

I tore out of Addison's arms and ran flat out down the trail, straight towards Abel's back.

He grunted when I slammed into his back and stopped walking when I wrapped my arms around his body and held on tightly to him.

"Let me go, Ariel." He growled low and dangerously at me.

I shivered, and not in a good way, at hearing his tone of voice, something I had never heard from him directed at me. And I sure as hell did not like hearing it now.

I held on to him tighter, refusing to let go, refusing to allow his tone of voice to frighten me away from him like I was sure he'd intended.

"No," I growled back just as fiercely as he had. Though, I was sure mine only came out sounding fierce to me and not to him. Voices were funny that way when they were your own. You always sounded different to yourself than you actually sounded out loud. "I will not let you go. Not now. Not ever. You need to talk to me."

"Ariel," Quinton shouted at me from somewhere behind, likely, not far enough behind because he'd never not follow me. Something I would usually have liked about him but at the moment I found it rather annoying. Why couldn't he just trust me enough to handle this situation? Why did he have to forcefully insert himself into everything? Normally, this might be okay, his forceful insertion of himself. But, tonight, with Abel? No, the only thing he was going to accomplish was pushing him further away than I had already done.

"Ariel," he ground out between clenched teeth. "I'm not messing around here with you."

I sighed.

I knew he wasn't and wasn't that just plain sad? I preferred him when he was being fun loving and carefree, always giving me shit about absolutely every tiny, little thing and never allowing me to get away with anything. So, why was it that he expected me to allow him to get away with this crap he was pulling? Was it because he was a guy and I was a girl? I certainly hoped not because finding that out would not make me happy.

"Quinton is going to kill me," Abel grunted under his breath.

He was right, of course. But what he failed to see or note was that I was certain *I* just might have to kill him first and he should at least be worried about me, too. He wasn't and I was overlooked as any sort of threat to him.

I didn't like this much either.

I didn't want to be underestimated or overlooked.

Not any more.

"Shut up, Abel," I whispered fiercely and his body jerked in my arms as if I'd struck him. "You're mad because I am not around the big house much anymore and you are upset and acting like a child because your feelings are hurt... or whatever. When you could have just said something sooner to me and we could have avoided all of this."

Oh, would you look at that, I was becoming more like an adult by the day.

Then, because I was who I was, I had to go ahead and ruin any sense of adulthood I had been going for. And I did it spectacularly.

"I don't even know why in the hell you'd think I would want

to spend time in that place ever, not after I've said several times just how much I did *not* want to be there," I told him honestly, not bothering to check my thoughts before I unleashed them out of my mouth.

Oh, shit.

Shit.

Shit.

Shit.

I should not have said that to him. I should never have said that at all.

I tried to repair the damage I had created.

"She's down there in the basement and I can't see past it whenever I'm there." I rushed out.

"You've been there several times when you came to see the Council member," he reminded me.

I had, this was no lie.

"Command performance," I immediately shot back. "I had no choice in that. Even Quinton told me I had no choice in that. That I either met Adrian at the big house or the cottage and he claimed I didn't want them, any of them, to be where I lived. I believed him and it's a decision I will stand by. I didn't want them in my home so I sucked the pain down and met them at the big house. If I didn't think it wasn't absolutely necessary then I would not have done it because I am so fucking uncomfortable even being in that house, it isn't even funny. That woman... Everything I learn about her makes me hate her even more than I already did before. It fills me up with hate inside and makes me sick to my stomach. I don't like feeling that way, it seriously hurts me, Abel. So, I don't go there unless I have to because of how it makes me feel."

His big body began to shake in my arms and I held on even tighter for fear of him trying to pull away from me in order to hide his emotions from me.

"Pretty girl," he whispered in a voice choked down with emotion.

I pressed my face into his back and inhaled his masculine scent. It comforted me enough to continue when I really didn't want to. I didn't want to talk anymore. I wanted this over with.

"If I still lived next door with Marcus then you guys would be coming to see me all the time. I just assumed it would be the same with me living at Dash's house. I figured if I didn't come here to see you then you would just show up at Dash's to see me. I'm so sorry I didn't think I should have been inviting you to come over all this time. It never even occurred to me to invite you over. I'm so sorry."

"I-" he said but stopped when a body slammed into my back and, because I held on so tightly to him, we both were propelled forward and taken down.

Abel's knees buckled and he went down face first into the dirt trail with me landing solidly on his back, with my arms still wrapped around his front. So my arms hit the dirt right before his face did. It didn't feel good to have my arms trapped beneath not only his body weight but my own.

And then there was the weight at my back, the added weight on top of my own.

I whimpered as I tried, and failed, to pull my arms out from underneath Abel. The noise came out high and whiney and very much not like my own voice.

The unknown person on top of me wrapped their arms not only around myself but around Abel as well. An Abel who was twitching and moaning in the dirt. I felt bad for him.

4

ARIEL

"Get off of her you damn fool," Quinton shouted from close by and I groaned.

Great. Just great.

He was not needed here for this particular situation. I thought it best that I handled this with only myself and the twins. I was actually glad to have Addison here with me to help me deal with his brother but Quinton I could for once do without.

"Make him stop," Abel whined from the bottom of the pile and I couldn't help the laughter that bubbled up and out of me. I was so happy to not be the only one who didn't want to deal with Quinton at the moment.

The arms around both Abel and myself tugged and we were both pulled backwards. It was awkward because we were laying down, but once the weight at my back moved away and only the arms around my shoulders remained it was easier to move. I rolled to my side and the arms were forced to release me. Since he was underneath me, they were forced to release Abel as well. I fell to my side in the dirt as Abel immediately rolled over to his front with his back now in the dirt too.

I gaped at him in shock as his robe flopped open and the entire front of his naked body was exposed to me.

"For Christ sakes," Quinton growled as hands went into my armpits and I was jerked up to my feet. "Cover yourself up."

Oh boy.

He didn't sound like he was mad. Oh no, for whatever reason, he sounded *enraged* and I didn't think this boded well for my Pepper twin.

Addison's grip on me tightened and he took a giant step back away from his twin, taking me, unfortunately, with him. I thought this was unfortunate because nobody else seemed to be able to calm Quint down or derail him like I could and I thought my Pepper twin could really use me as a buffer at a time like this.

I was also mildly alarmed at the fact Addison was so ready to leave his brother behind to face Quinton's rage all alone. This didn't sit well with me. They were supposed to be a team! One, singular unit!

Abel clutched his robe tightly shut as he climbed to his feet. Once he stood tall he started to brush the dirt off of the front of his robe. Though, from what I'd seen, the majority of the dirt had clung to his chest and um... other places and he'd need to reopen the robe in order to get all of the dirt off of himself.

"Addison," I whispered urgently as he took us another step back and farther away from his brother. "I don't think now is the time to abandon him."

His mouth came to my ear where he whispered, "We aren't abandoning him, Ariel. We're just moving you back out of the way from Quinton's wrath."

I didn't think this was a wise idea either and it sure felt like we were abandoning his brother in his time of need.

"Addison," I whispered his name in protest. He let me get out no more.

He shook me violently in his arms and whispered harshly, "Quiet."

I didn't much care for this either and my heart inside my chest squeezed painfully at seeing Abel standing by his own, facing off an angry Quinton.

Addison dragged me back another step. Then another. He didn't stop until we were several feet away from them. Once we were at what, I was assuming he felt a safe distance, he let me go and moved around me. He put his warm palm in my stomach and pushed lightly, gently.

His blue eyes scorched into mine and I caught my breath at the determination and resolve in his eyes. A muscle in his jaw ticked angrily but his voice was surprisingly gentle when he spoke to me.

"You stay here," he said in his quiet but gentle voice. "No matter what happens, pretty girl, you stay here. You stay out of it."

I bit my lip hard as I nodded my head in ascent.

His eyes roamed over my face before he sighed heavily. That sigh spoke volumes and I knew just by hearing it that he didn't believe in my nod and he didn't believe for a hot second that I'd stay where he'd put me, that I'd stay out of it. And he would be right.

His hand went to the back of my neck and he pulled me forward as he bent down. He kissed my forehead sweetly before letting me go and turning back to head towards his brother. I guessed that was his way of forgiving me for not listening to him. Or, so I told myself.

My eyes widened in shock as I watched in horror as Quinton put his hand in Abel's shoulder and forcefully shoved him. He pushed so hard that Abel went back on a foot.

"Quinton," I whispered in horror. "Stop it."

Addison made it to his brothers' side and crossed his arms over his chest.

"Don't put your hands on him in anger ever again, Quint," He snarled angrily. He moved into his brothers' side, not stopping until their sides were touching.

I had to say, I was in agreement with Addison on this one because I, too, had not liked seeing Quint put his hands-on Abel in such a way. Violence was never the answer. Unless, of course, you were throwing a rock at some stubborn fool's head. Well, maybe even then it wasn't entirely okay but who are you to judge me.

Quinton pointed his fist in Abel's direction and snarled at Addison, "He fucking ruined Halloween for her and he doesn't deserve to stay here and enjoy the rest of the night with her. Not when he fucked up so badly. It's not just his relationship with her that's been put in jeopardy by his behavior, or even your own. It's not just about the two of you. It's about the rest of us as well. Your actions," Quint jabbed his fist again at Abel for emphasis, "*his* actions, don't just have consequences for the two of you but have the potential to ruin it for the rest of us. You both need to take that into account before you do anything. I'm not-"

I'd had more than enough of this bull crap and decided to tell him.

Well, given the rest of the guys who'd moved over to watch the show and away from the fire, I guess you could say I'd decided to tell them all what was what.

I did not enjoy the fact I now had a bigger audience than I would have liked. I wanted to just deal with this with the twins and not the rest of them but I didn't always get what I wanted. Like having a fun Halloween. That was now right down the shitter and getting worse by the second.

"Shut up," I yelled at Quinton and it felt like the entire woods froze at the words that were wrenched out of me.

I could feel their eyes on me from behind, burning into me, and I saw that the three of them standing in front of me only had eyes for me as well.

I didn't bother to look away from Quinton since my words were for him. Though, they were aimed at all of them and I hoped like hell they all took them in.

"You're being an asshole," I said quietly. Okay, so, perhaps that part was simply for Quinton. "And you're wrong. Absolutely, without a doubt in my mind, *wrong.* There are going to be certain aspects to my relationship with the others that have not one thing to do with you or anybody else. Admittedly, things got out of control tonight."

I winced as I said this and hurried along to get out the rest when Quinton's eyes widened alarmingly and his mouth dropped open.

Nuh uh. No way was I letting him take over this particular conversation.

"But, if you'd have left it alone and given me time and space I would have had it under control." Okay, so that part might not have been entirely true but we'd never know because he hadn't given me a chance to figure it out. "Instead you just barged in on our conversation, tried to boss everyone around, like usual, and ended up making everything worse. When things didn't need to have gone in that direction at all."

Quinton let out a humorless laugh and asked, "Are you fucking serious right now with this, Ariel?"

Actually, as much as I wanted to be right, I wasn't entirely sure that I was. And I really didn't like it when he used my name as opposed to baby. It usually meant he was going to verbally lay me out and it wasn't ever pleasant for me or enjoyable.

"Ariel," Abel said my name kindly. "I don't think you should be-"

My head slowly swiveled in his direction and I barked out, "No," cutting him off.

"Babe," Quinton said but I didn't listen to him either.

I shook my head. "You tried to send him to his room like a naughty child because you thought he hurt my feelings or whatever. Quinton, that is beyond messed up. He's not an errant child. He's a member of this coven just the same as you are, just the same as everyone else and I don't think it's right the way you treated him. And, I also don't think it's right that you didn't trust me enough to fix the situation and smooth things out with him on my own."

Quinton's entire face softened and he muttered, "Christ, baby. I trust you."

I shook my head as I felt tears sting the backs of my eyes. I didn't think he trusted me, not how I trusted him. I didn't even feel better about him calling me baby again, it did nothing to soothe my frayed nerves or tattered emotions.

"I don't-"

"It's not about you," Julian said as his immense heat moved into my side. He put an arm around my waist and pulled me into his body. I moved into him easily and my hand came up to rest on his middle. Too late I realized it was his *bare* middle. I sucked in a sharp breath as my hand encountered soft hair and I froze.

I tilted my head back to look up at him to see him not looking down at my face but at where I'd placed my hand instead with a strange, small smile on his face. I fought the urge to look at where I'd placed my hand as well and, fortunately or unfortunately, depending on how you looked at it, I won.

"Julian," I muttered in embarrassment. Thankfully, I no longer felt like crying.

His eyes slid to mine and his small, strange smile turned into a full-fledged one as his hand around my waist slid down to my hip and he trailed his finger tips over the edge of my cotton undies.

"Really, Jules?" Quinton said tiredly. "You're going to feel her up right here in front of the rest of us while we're having a drama to end all drama's?"

I sucked in a sharp breath and heat hit my back.

Damien.

If he minded that Julian's arm was in between our bodies at my back he didn't show it. In fact, he wrapped an arm around Julian's shoulders and pulled him tighter into my body as he wrapped his other arm around my middle, just below my breasts.

I watched Quinton as his eyes followed every single movement. They heated, burning brighter by the second and any hint of hostility or anger slid right off of his face.

Oh boy.

Things were getting dangerously out of my control here. Not, that I was fooled into thinking I'd ever really held much control to begin with, but I'd at least had some over my own damn body.

"Don't we have a ritual to participate in?" I blurted in a high, almost shrill voice.

The hair at my back was swept to the side and over my right shoulder. A warm, wet tongue flicked out before lips met my neck right below my ear.

I shivered pleasantly.

"Dame," Julian muttered under his breath. "I don't think this is the way to go when we're all mostly naked."

My head twisted and I looked at Julian with big eyes and parted lips.

He chuckled softly. "Right," he said in a quiet voice. "I won't talk about being naked anymore and I won't mention the fact that if you were to slide your hand down six more inches you'd encounter something hard and all for you."

I gasped as I immediately removed my hand from his stomach.

Damien laughed and I felt his body shaking behind me.

"I think you're scaring her, Jules." Damien told his roommate.

"Both of you, knock it off," Quinton snapped at them but his voice was lacking it's usual heat or anger. "Let's leave her alone with the twins to sort out their shit while we make sure the fire didn't burn out."

"It didn't burn out," I heard Tyson say but I was too embarrassed to turn and look at him.

"If anything it got hotter," Dash remarked quietly.

Damien leaned back into me again and gently nipped at my neck with his teeth before his palm flattened over top of my underwear and he gave me a one armed hug. Julian grunted and I knew Damien had hugged him tighter as well. Then he let me go and his heat at my back was suddenly gone.

Julian took his cue from Damien, gave my hip a gentle squeeze before letting me go as well and his heat was gone just as fast as Damien's had left me.

I looked over my shoulder in time to see the backs of four hooded cloaked individuals as they walked away from me.

I felt bereft without their heat engulfing me and I missed them as soon as they were gone. But I had bigger things to deal with, like the emotional mess that had been created between myself and my Pepper twin. And, then there was Quinton's aggressive behavior that he'd suddenly dropped but that didn't mean I'd just stopped being pissy towards him because he'd had a sudden change of heart.

I was a girl.

It didn't always work that way.

Quinton paused at my side briefly before walking away and heading back towards the fire.

"I fucked this up," he said. "But I trust you to fix it. Bring them back to the fire with you when you're done here, will you?"

Then he was gone.

I wanted to punch him.

"So," Abel said and he cleared his throat. "You saw my dick again."

I gasped. "I did not see your dick before tonight," I said in outrage even though this might have been a lie. I had seen one of them naked below the waist before in a situation where they'd also been wearing robes and nothing else.

"If it was bigger then it was my dick she saw, twin, not yours," Addison told his brother seriously.

I groaned loudly, knowing things here would slowly deteriorate and they'd be ribbing each other hard in no time, both of them jonesing to be the hotter, better twin. I didn't get it and never did when they started up with this nonsense.

"Guys," I said slowly but loudly, really not wanting to discuss this particular topic any longer.

They completely ignored me and carried on like I wasn't even there.

"Bullshit," Abel shot back. "Mine's the bigger one."

I sighed.

"Maybe we should just ask her," Addison suggested and they both finally turned to me almost like they'd just remembered they weren't alone and I was standing there.

"Ariel," Abel said seriously as he walked towards me with his hands held out at his sides. I tried not to look any lower than his face.

"No," I said, not caring about what he was going to say or ask me. "I don't want to hear about your dicks anymore."

Addison followed his brothers' footsteps and headed my

way. "No?" he asked quietly and I flushed again. "Maybe you just want to see them?"

I shook my head. They were making this horrible for me.

"Do you guys want to spend the night with me?" I asked them in a change of subject. I didn't ask just to change the subject but because I really did miss them and wanted to spend more time with them.

"You don't need to-" Abel said seriously as he stopped directly in front of me. He lowered his arms to his side and his robe finally closed again.

"You're right," I cut him off to say. "I don't have to do anything. I actually want to spend time with you. But, I don't want you to get upset with me because I want to spend time with the both of you. Are you going to get mad because I don't want just you but your brother as well?"

His hand came up and he cupped my jaw sweetly. His green eyes glowed in the moonlight and shined with an ethereal light.

"I'm sorry," he murmured. "I was insecure and stupid and let it get the better of me because I missed you. I love that you're as into my twin as you are me. That's exactly what we need in our partner. You're exactly what we need."

Addison moved into his twin and wrapped his arm around his shoulders and hung off of him.

"He's right, you know," Addison told me. "Still, my dick's bigger."

I couldn't help it even if I tried. I threw my head back and burst out laughing.

I didn't know that the sound carried all the way to where the others stood around the fire and each and every single one of them smiled at hearing it.

5

ARIEL

"Make it burn, pretty girl."

I turned to see Addison standing beside me. He'd said exactly what his brother had said to me, something he hadn't been close enough to have heard. I shivered as his sky blue eyes burned through me.

I didn't question him repeating his twins' words, they were odd but so was I and I loved them for their differences.

The fire blazed high in the metal barrel as we stood around it in a wide circle. I was also choosing to ignore the little fact that some of their robes were hanging open and not a single one of them had the same qualms about nudity as I did because, from what I'd seen, not a single one of those guys had a single stitch of clothing on underneath those robes. I'd been embarrassed at first. But I was choosing to ignore that as well. I didn't want to be a prude and make them feel uncomfortable about their traditions and I didn't want to further taint this night I'd been allowed to participate in. They'd let me in their inner circle, finally, and I didn't want to muck it up any more than I already had.

I raised my hand and flung it back out in the direction of the barrel, flinging part of my energy with it. I saw in my mind's eye the flame shoot up high, racing towards the sky. The flame shot up and the guys raised their arms towards the sky along with it.

I shivered pleasantly as a warm wind blew past my cheeks and ruffled my hair. My hood flew back with the wind and my cheeks finally burned due to warmth instead of embarrassment.

All around the circle the guys had their hoods blown back and off of their heads. Their arms were out at their sides and their faces were upturned, looking up at the moons brightness.

"Imagine, pretty girl," Addison said from beside me. "A flow of energy that starts at the top of your head and slowly moves down towards the bottom of your feet. It's a pure, white energy. A cleansing energy, if you will. Imagine it filling you up on the inside."

I tilted my head back towards the brightly lit open sky and did exactly as Addison instructed me to.

My soul lightened and I felt better than I ever had before. Freer, lighter, yet, finally full to bursting with something so pure, so beautiful, I couldn't find words to describe it.

"Amazing," I whispered in awe.

Addison chuckled and I knew he'd heard my whispered word.

"We must give part of it back," Abel said from the other side of me. "We cannot take this much without giving back. It's selfish and you must never use magic without it taking something from you in return."

I heard something like this before from them. All magic came with a price and some times that price could be hefty. Usually, it was a drain on your energy.

"How do we-" I started to ask but was shushed by one of the twins.

"You listen," Addison told me. "And you follow Quinton's lead."

I looked away from the bright, night sky then to look across the barrel of fire to Quinton who was directly across from me. For once, he wasn't paying attention to me. Like everyone else, he had his head thrown back and tipped up at the sky with his arms out spread at his sides. A look of complete rapture and adoration filled his face and my lips parted at the beauty I saw there. I'd never seen him look so free before either.

My eyes roamed around the circle to take in the others and I was blown away to see that same look from surly Uncle Quinton's face graced the other's faces as well.

Dash's face held no hint of the pain it usually held. And he didn't look closed off at all but was instead open and carefree. My heart filled with joy at the sight.

Tyson's face was open, soft and there was no simmering rage beneath the surface. A miraculous feat I had never seen before. My heart warmed further at seeing it.

Julian looked at peace. There was no calculation or mirth behind his soft smile. I hadn't realized until that moment that I had never noticed the calculation in his eyes before until it was actually missing. I wasn't frightened by learning this information, but rather I was excited to see him as he was now, without the friendly mask he usually hid behind. This new look into him elated me. It also hurt my heart to see he'd hid behind a mask that I'd never even known was there before. I vowed to dig deeper into this side to him as soon as I got the chance to.

Damien, for the first time since I'd ever met him unless we were having a private moment between the two of us, looked open and vulnerable. He didn't do well with vulnerability, I knew, but he seemed to give it freely out here. My breath caught in my throat at the sight of it, something that told me he was more comfortable with showing his vulnerable side around his brothers than he probably ever would be showing me. I was okay with this, he had his male pride to cater to and I would never undermine that. He was incredibly sweet. Though, I was certain I would be amongst the very few who ever described him as such.

I looked to the person closest to my right side then immediately looked to the person closest to me on the left. Addison and Abel. Neither of them were focused on the moon shining bright in the sky but, instead, were focused on me but pretending like they weren't. Their eyes skirted to the side and away from me as soon as I glanced in their directions.

It didn't feel right to me that they were more focused on me instead of being focused on what we were all supposed to be taking part of.

I felt too good to worry about them and their worry for me at the moment, though. I couldn't do it when my body was full of bliss thanks to the moon and I focused back on Quinton standing across the fire from me.

"My mistress, the moon," Quinton shouted up at the sky and the fire shot higher than it ever had before. It was almost as if it was reaching for the moon itself.

I felt the beautiful, light energy inside me reach up at the same time the flames did at hearing his words. They, too, were reaching for the moon and I didn't have to question it this time because I felt it deep inside me where I fancied my soul took up space.

"We open our circle to you and we give thanks to thee," Quinton cried into the night.

Everyone inside the circle besides myself repeated his words on a shout.

No one had told me I needed to repeat after Quinton so I hadn't known to do it. I really hoped I didn't mess things up here and would be sure to participate the next time words were shouted at the sky.

"We raise our arms and draw down the power of our beautiful mistress, the moon."

I repeated the words on a shout along with the rest of our circle.

I felt a shift in the circle, a gentle breeze pushing me towards the right, and I didn't hesitate to follow it in that direction. I followed behind Abel's back as he moved, following behind his brothers.

"Mother Earth, we give our thanks."

We repeated the words and I could swear the ground rumbled beneath my feet.

"Sacred Air, we honor thee."

I sucked in a sharp breath as wind slapped me harshly in the face and my hair blew out straight behind my head. Still, I kept moving in the circle and chanting along with the rest of my coven.

"Spirit, we embolden thee."

I stumbled and missed my chance at repeating Quinton's words when I felt like a significant piece of me raised from my chest before slamming back down inside of me.

Hands met with my hips and I was lifted back into place in the circle and, at gentle urging from the twin behind me, pushed forward and back into line.

"Fire, we respect thee!"

My entire body felt like I'd walked through a ring of fire and I'd received a sunburn. Oddly, it wasn't an unpleasant feeling, but merely a tightening of my skin.

"Water, we worship thee."

Thunder rumbled in the sky before a light sprinkling of rain fell down upon us. Oddly enough, this did not touch the fire in any way and it seemed to blaze brighter than ever.

The rain immediately stopped as did the twin in front of me, causing me to jerk to a stop. Everyone turned to face the fire again and I turned with them. They lowered their hands with their palms facing down flat towards the ground. I mimicked their movements.

"We appreciate the gifts you've generously given us tonight," Quinton said in subdued voice that was at odds with his earlier shouting. "But we are not a selfish coven and we understand the gift we've been given and choose to give back to our sacred Mother Earth."

The magic and heat swirling around inside of me had me in complete agreement with him. We needed to give back to something, I didn't care what it was we gave back too, though. I just knew that I felt far too full and if I didn't get rid of some of this energy soon I'd likely burst."

"Mother Earth," Quinton said in a clear voice. "Take what you will from us."

I felt energy leech out of my hands and I shivered, not liking this part of the experience. It had been all good up until this point, enjoyable even.

But this? Giving back? It didn't feel all that good when I'd much rather keep it all to myself.

Magic, I was learning, wasn't always fun and games.

Sometimes it sucked the joy right out of you.

Literally.

Why did everything have to come with a price, especially when it felt good?

6

ARIEL

I blew out a heavy breath as I forced my shoulders to relax and the tension out of my body. I couldn't hide out in the bathroom for forever like a coward. It was a sleep over, something I'd done before with them, I had nothing to be nervous about.

On that one, I opened the door and exited the bathroom.

The Salt and Pepper twins had decided, upon my invitation, to come home with me. I hadn't bothered to ask Dash if he cared if they stayed the night. He'd told me over and over again that it was my house too and I needed to treat it as such. He wasn't my parent, he was my roommate and one of my boyfriends, I didn't need to ask him if I could have people sleep over. It would make him feel badly if I asked, like he was failing at making me feel at home.

I hesitated in the hallway, listening. The twins could be heard quietly murmuring from inside my bedroom as well as the tv in the background. That wasn't what I was listening for though. The rest of the house seemed quiet, empty, and I didn't think Dash had made it home just yet. The twins and I hadn't stuck around after the ritual, instead choosing to change quickly and get the heck out of there. Quinton had watched us leave with a tight mouth and narrowed eyes. But he'd let us leave without making a peep which I thought was wise on his behalf. After sifting through the shit in the closet that I had assumed I would never wear, I found a t-shirt and jeans to put on instead of that ancient dress again. I'd hung the dress up and left it in the closet. I'd kept the boots, though. I wasn't ready to part with those just yet. What could I say, I seemed to have a fondness for shoes and boots and the guys seemed to like buying them for me. It was the one thing I seemed to be okay with indulging in.

A black bundle of fur rubbed up against my ankle and I grinned down at Binx, Dash's cat. I grinned down at him as I bent down and gave him a quick scratch behind his ears. He immediately started purring.

I shook my head before leaving him alone in the hallway. If he wanted to follow me then he would. Otherwise, he'd sit in Dash's doorway waiting for him to come home. He was an odd little creature which is why I didn't pick him up and carry him into my bedroom with me. He was particular when it came to the guys and, often times, moody around them. One day he could love one of them then the next he'd hiss angrily at them and maybe even scratch them if they got too close to him. He'd never once hissed at me and I'd never seen him hiss at Dash, either. He seemed to love Dash and I wholeheartedly and I loved him fiercely right back. I loved him as if he were my own little bundle of furry love and I feared if things ever went south with Dash and I was forced to move out I would be taking the cat with me. I'd steal him if I had to.

He meowed pathetically at my departing back but didn't follow behind me. I looked over my shoulder to see him prance to Dash's open doorway where he plopped down like he was guarding the entrance against unwanted guests. His tail swished back and forth, slowly, in agitation.

"Weirdo," I muttered as I walked into my bedroom.

"Is Dash home?" Abel asked quietly and my head snapped up in time to see him sit up quickly on my wicker love seat. He was shirtless and only wearing a pair of black boxers on his body.

Heat hit my cheeks as my brain immediately went to what I'd seen earlier, him being naked and my eyes skirted away from him.

The sight that greeted me on my bed wasn't a whole lot better than the one on the love seat because Addison was wearing matching boxers as Abel and he was sprawled out shirtless on his back on my bed.

They were so big that the both of them being here half naked in my bedroom made my room seem like it was a whole lot smaller than it really was because they took up so much space. They made the room seem suddenly suffocating. Or, maybe it was because the room had suddenly seemed to be twelve hundred degrees and I was on the verge of fainting. I waived my hand at my face to cool it off. I didn't help me in the slightest. Perhaps I should have taken a cold shower instead of simply changing into my pajamas.

"No," I croaked out in answer to Abel's question. I cleared my throat and shared, "I was talking to Binx. He was waiting for me outside of the bathroom."

They both grunted in unison and I assumed it meant that they were agreeing on something that had to do with my sweet little cat.

Addison stood up from the bed in one fluid movement. He pulled the comforter and top sheet back. He slid under the covers and climbed back into bed. He laid his head back on one of my many pillows and pulled the blanket up his chest.

"I'm tired," he mumbled. "I know we should probably stay up until Dash at least gets home but I don't want to stay up. I'm not trying to be selfish, I'm just tired. I didn't sleep well last night and the day has really started wearing on me."

I studied him and he did look tired. There were dark smudges underneath his eyes that I hadn't noticed earlier. His eyelids drooped as he put his hands behind his head, making his muscles bulge.

I imagined my face turned even brighter as I watched him.

"You sleep, twin," Abel muttered. "I'll stay awake and make sure it's all good when Dash gets home."

I frowned at him.

"I don't understand," I said in confusion. "Why does someone need to stay awake until Dash comes home?"

I yawned and opened my mouth so wide my jaw cracked. I was as tired as Addison was because he wasn't wrong when he'd said it was a long day and I was beat.

Holidays were fun and I couldn't wait to do Christmas with the guys, but they were also exhausting and I had a feeling Christmas was going to be a whole lot more so than Halloween had been. I absolutely could not wait.

"Get in bed," Abel ordered.

I shot him a dirty look but did what he'd told me to do. I was too tired to argue with him. Addison held the covers back for me and I slid in bed beside him.

"What do you guys want to watch?" Abel asked quietly and I finally noticed what was playing on the television that had been mounted to the wall in the corner of the room. A television I hadn't originally wanted but now left on with the sleep timer on every night when I went to bed. I'd so far watched all of *Friday Night Lights* and had since moved on to the DVD's of *The L Word* that Damien had gotten for me. He'd gotten me so many different DVD's of different television shows that Julian had picked up shelves for me that were mounted to the wall in the corner underneath the tv. I hadn't bothered arguing with him about how I could have easily put them on my book shelf with my books because there was no point in arguing with them when it came to them buying things for me. I'd long since given up that battle because it was one I knew I couldn't win.

However deep I was into *The L Word* and wasn't interested in jumping from show to show because I preferred to binge watch them until I was all caught up on the episodes, that didn't mean I wanted to watch it with the twins.

"Something with vampires," Addison muttered and I turned my head on the pillow to stare at him in surprise.

"You like vampires?" I asked him curiously. This wasn't something I'd known about him before. In fact, I think I sucked in the girlfriend department because I didn't know much about their likes and interests. Outside of me, I knew they liked me.

"He likes anything supernatural," Abel told me and I looked to him on the couch.

"Do you like anything supernatural as well?" I asked him.

"No," Addison answered for his twin.

Huh. It seemed they didn't have similar interests after all. I certainly hadn't expected Addison to tell me he was into all things supernatural. I couldn't see him with *Twilight* posters up in his room and I *really* couldn't see him enjoying watching sparkly vampires.

Abel got up off the couch and dropped to his knees in front of the shelves below the mounted television.

"Abel," I called softly. "Just pick out something that you'd like to watch. Your brother doesn't look like he's going to stay up for long enough to enjoy whatever it is that you put on. I don't think I'll be far behind him. So, pick out whatever you want. You're going to be the only person who really ends up watching it."

I was curious to see what he'd pick out from my many

DVD's. Of course, I only owned the one's Damien had picked out for me, but I didn't imagine they would have been much different if it had been me who'd picked them out, but only when it came to the one's I'd actually seen before. Which, wasn't many of them, if I was being honest.

"Come here, pretty girl," Addison rumbled as his arm slid underneath me and around my shoulders.

I turned on my side and curled into his big, warm body. He wrapped his arm tightly around my middle as I snuggled into him, resting my head on his shoulder. I groaned happily as his heat engulfed me. I absolutely loved the way I felt whenever one of the guys had their arms wrapped around me. I felt safe, secure and like I was finally home. It was the best feeling in the universe.

I had never once felt safe until I'd entered their world and they'd sweetly wrapped me up in their heat.

"*Pretty Little Liars,* it is." Abel said triumphantly.

I smirked at Addison and asked, "Have you seen this show before?"

I had to admit, I was curious. I hadn't watched it myself yet because they looked like stuck up girls and I thought I'd be able to relate better with a girl who'd lost a whole lot, just found out she had magic, and couldn't seem to find a place or time to catch her own breath and was constantly drowning in the world around her. I actually got *that.*

"Nope." Addison told me.

I smiled at him as I rolled back on to my back, leaving my head on his shoulder. I threw my right leg in-between his thighs and tangled it with his legs. His hand came to my stomach, going around my hip and immediately under and up my tank top.

I sucked in a sharp breath as heat scorched its way up my

middle. He pulled my shirt up with his hand and it didn't stop until my shirt was half way up my back.

The front door slammed shut, making me jump and Addison pressed his hand into my back, pushing me deeper into him.

"I bet that's Dash," I heard Abel say and I heard the love seat shift under his weight as he stood up. "I will go check and then I'll be right back. We'll start the show as soon as I get back. Are either of you hungry?"

I groaned at the thought of putting any more food inside my poor, poor stomach. I was also surprised I didn't have a stomach ache after all the candy Quinton had forced me to consume throughout the day.

Both twins chuckled at me.

"So, no food," Abel stated, sounding clearly amused. "I thought you were going to throw up after he made you eat those mini candy bars."

I groaned again and pressed my forehead deeper into Addison's shoulder. I desperately wanted Abel to stop talking about stupid candy.

"Twin?"

"Nothing for me, twin." Addison rumbled. "I didn't eat as much candy as our girl here did, but if I eat another sweet thing I think I might fall into a sugar induced coma."

Abel chuckled.

"Right," he said. "I think it's going to take us a whole week of working out just to burn all that shit off."

I put my hands on Addison's stomach and pushed myself away from him, far enough away so I could look him in the eye.

"You guys work out?" I asked him stupidly. I had my hands all over hard muscle! Of course they worked out.

"Of course we do, pretty girl," Abel remarked and I turned my head to the side to see him looking down at me with a sweet, soft look on his face. Oh boy. I was betting he got that lovely look on his face because he really liked seeing me in bed with his brother.

He ran his hand down the center of his chest, not stopping until his palm rested flat and covered up his belly button. "We don't want all of this to turn to fat. We need to stay nice and hard. The girls like it like that."

He had that last part right.

"Leave her be," Addison said to his brother. "She doesn't need any more of that kind of talk tonight. She had enough in the field."

Abel's face didn't lose the soft look but the corners of his lips curled upwards in the ghost of a grin. I was more than pleased when he left it at that and, after shaking his head, he continued on his way out of my room.

"We don't have much time," Addison muttered before his hand that was up my shirt at my back came back around to my front and he gently pushed me back. My back met with the mattress and I looked up into the serious, sky blue eyes of my Salt twin.

"Much time for what?" I asked in a hushed voice that stated clearly that this was the last thing I'd expected out of him.

He put his elbow into the bed and sat up, leaning over me.

"The first time I kiss you," he muttered as his eyes dropped down to my lips. "I wanted it to be just the two of us. I know how my brother and I are and I know this might seem a little out of the norm from what you'd expect from us, but this is really important to me. I know my brother and I know he will likely need some one-on-one time with you and just him in the near future. But he won't care if he doesn't kiss you in front of me or not. I know he made a big deal earlier about wanting to separate himself from me but, in the end, it comes down to the fact the two of us shared a womb together and, no matter what happens, it'll always be the two of us together facing off everything else."

His words didn't relax me but instead made the opposite happen, they made me tense. I had always seen them as a duo, the ultimate package... together no matter what. This entire day had been a serious eye opener for me, to say the least.

So, was there a chance they could be separated, one twin without the other? Because, if so, I wanted absolutely no part of that. Did I want one if I couldn't have the other? Sure, but only because the both of them meant so much to me that I'd take them any way I could get them. The thought of only one of them wanting me scared the absolute crap right out of me. I really didn't see them as separate any more, they were one to me and that's how I liked it.

"But-" I opened my mouth to tell him that I might have been in love with him and his brother but I didn't ever want to choose between them. I'd also kind of been fantasizing about being with the both of them at the same time, which was something I wasn't about to be embarrassed about because I would never, not ever, be telling another living, breathing soul about my fantasies. Especially since the only people I knew in my life were my guys and they would just laugh their asses off at me and use it to embarrass me as often as they could.

No thanks. I would be passing on all of that outrageous nonsense.

"No buts," Addison murmured with his eyes on my lips. He bit his bottom lip before his eyes lifted to my own and he released his lower lip. "Do you not want to kiss me, pretty girl?"

I nodded my head because I absolutely did. I wanted all of them to kiss me more and I wanted them to touch me like I was their girlfriend. Instead, I was stuck with a bunch of boyfriends who almost seemed afraid to touch me. It seemed absolutely absurd to be a girl who had seven boyfriends but couldn't get a single one of them to get to third base with. It was beginning to become maddening.

I wanted to kiss him just as much as I wanted to kiss his brother. They were both easy on the eyes and deliciously large. I absolutely loved how much bigger their bodies were than my own. I loved that Addison's thigh was at least twice the size of my own. I love that his hips were wider than mine, his stomach thicker. I loved how much harder than my body his was. They were both hot. They were all hot.

And I was...not.

It bothered me.

I had never been proud of my scars or had ever tried to show them off before because I didn't want attention drawn to them. I also didn't go out of my way to hide them. I wore tank tops all the time, I just never worried about people noticing my scars before because I never allowed anyone to get close enough to me to get a good look at them. Now I had one I had to wear for the rest of my life on my face. I usually didn't think about that one either, the horror of that one had worn off weeks after I'd received it. Mostly, because the rest of the guys had let it go after I'd seemed to accept it. As soon as they'd gotten over it and stopped mentioning it I had stopped thinking about it all the time. I had mean scars. *Loads* of them. One more didn't mean anything to me, even when I was forced to wear it on my face.

I only cared when I thought they would care. As soon as I realized they only cared out of feeling guilty for possibly being to blame, I got over it. I didn't think most of them even saw the scar when they looked at my face. I saw it, looking back at me in the mirror every time I got a good look at my face.

I knew it marred my good looks.

I wanted to be pretty for them because they deserved to have a girl that at least looked good. But, they had me and they thought I did look good.

I decided it was best not to argue with them because it seemed stupid to do so. Still, that didn't mean I didn't sometimes feel badly on the inside because I felt like they deserved better than me, and not just because I now had a scar on my face.

"Addison," I whispered his name.

"No," he said quietly but firmly.

Eyes intent, he leaned down and pressed his lips to mine.

At first contact I whimpered and raised my hand to the back of his head. I ran my fingers through his white blonde hair as his tongue slipped inside my mouth for the first time.

While staying propped up with his elbows on the mattress, he lowered the bottom half of his body down on top of mine. We were hips to hips, thighs to thighs. Though, his thighs engulfed my own. The same with his hips. I didn't mind, I loved the feel of his weight on top of my own.

He kissed me. It was deep and intense. My fingers in his hair tightened the longer the kiss went on. I couldn't help it, I needed something to hold on to.

He moaned into my mouth when I pulled on his hair and I turned my head to the side, breaking the kiss.

"Am I hurting you?" I asked breathlessly.

"No," he whispered. "I like it."

I kind of did too, which surprised me.

His bottom lip brushed against mine and his tongue came out to brush gently across the top part of my bottom lip.

"Open," he whispered and I did as I was told, opening my mouth for him.

We kissed and he slowly lowered the upper half of his body down on top of mine. Somehow though he managed to do it and not smother me at the same time. Hands now free because they were no longer keeping him off of me, his hand came up to cup my jaw while we kissed. The other hand went to my side and up underneath my shirt. It didn't stop its upwards travel until he made it to my bra. Then, not messing around in the slightest, his hand slid underneath my bra and he pushed it up off of my breast.

I sucked in a sharp breath as I twisted my head to the side and his lips left my own.

"Addison," I whimpered as his thumb brushed over my puckered nipple.

He chuckled darkly. "Yeah," he said. "I like it when you say my name all breathy like that."

I had to admit, I liked it too.

"Am I interrupting something," A bored voice called from behind Addison and I gasped. The actual voice didn't register, just the words.

I let go of Addison's hair and dropped my hands down to his shoulders. I pushed on him and whispered in horror, "Get off of me, right this second."

"Pretty girl," he whispered in a soft, sweet voice. "It's alright. It's just Abel."

That relaxed me, only a fraction though, and I stopped pressing against his shoulders to get him to get off of me.

The bed dipped and I turned my head on the pillow to the side. Abel had sat on the bed beside us. He brought his hand to my face and ran his thumb gently across the apple of my cheek. Over my scar. His eyes didn't track the movement, his thumb moved on its own memory. It was sweet and I relaxed entirely.

It used to bother me when they touched my scar. Now I saw it as sweet, and I knew Quinton touched it to remind himself that it was there and he needed to take better care of me. That was his way of thinking. He hated that scar, but not because he thought it made me ugly. He hated it because he thought it meant he'd failed at his job in protecting me. I didn't like his way of thinking but I no longer argued with him about it.

"Abel?" I asked quietly.

I was worried about him after what had happened in the woods with him earlier. I was terrified of his reaction to witnessing his brother with his hand up my shirt and his tongue in my mouth.

His eyes dropped to said mouth before lifting back to my eyes.

"Will it freak you out if I kiss you now?" He asked me.

My eyes widened in surprise at this question. It wouldn't freak me out so I shook my head, mutely answering him.

He grinned as he leaned into his brothers' side and his head descended towards mine. His green eyes shone brightly in the dark room before his lips brushed against mine in a gentle kiss.

Abel kissed me while Addison used his knee to push my legs apart. His hips dropped between my legs once he had them spread far enough apart to get in between them. He immediately pushed up against me with his hardness and I heard him groan.

My shirt slid up my stomach and up over my bra that had been pushed up off of both of my breasts. My breasts were exposed and, before I had the chance to freak out about it, Addison cupped my breasts in his hands and something warm and wet ran over my nipple. His mouth latched onto my nipple and he sucked. Hard.

I cried out and suddenly Abel was no longer kissing me. His head was turned as he looked over his shoulder at what his brother was doing.

"Stop," Abel said in a hoarse voice. "Twin, you have to stop now."

The wet heat left my puckered nipple and I shivered as the air hit it.

"I don't want to," Addison rumbled.

"I know," Abel told his twin. "I don't want to either, but we have to. We promised we would take things slow with her. Ty promised us he'd do the same. That way we are all on the same page when it happens."

I pushed Abel out of the way and sat up. I quickly tugged my top down to cover my naked breasts. I had to reach under my top to drag my bra back down into place.

"Just take it off," Addison said from where his head sat in my lap.

I frowned down at him before reaching around to the back of my bra where the clasp was and unhooking it. I pulled my arms into my tank top and took my bra off underneath my shirt. I dropped it onto Addison's face and shoved my arms back through the proper holes.

"What are you talking about?" I asked them.

They had promised to take things slow with me? And they hadn't included me in the discussion. I wondered if they knew what had happened between myself and Tyson and what they would think about it.

"I'm tired," Addison rushed out. He quickly sat up, pulling his head out of my lap.

He fell to his back in the bed, put his arm underneath my back and hauled me up against his body. I curled into him and threw my thigh over top of his and snuggled into his side.

The blankets behind me lifted and heat hit my back. Abel's arm went around my side as his body made contact with my back. He didn't stop with just me, though, and his arm went around his brother as well. He placed his palm above where mine was pressed into his stomach.

They were so weird.

I freaking loved it.

"Sleep, pretty girl." One of them commanded. I didn't know which one because I wasn't looking at them to see whose mouth moved when the words came out.

I had questions. Plenty of them. And I wanted answers but I

was smart enough to know that they weren't going to answer my questions. Not unless they wanted to and it was clear from their sudden behavior that they had no desire to answer me.

I was screwed until I could corner Uncle Quint and press him for answers. He was my go to source for information.

7

ARIEL

I jerked awake with a start and immediately felt trapped. I tried to roll to the side in order to untangle myself from Addison but was held firmly in place by more than one set of arms. Addison was in front of me, or, more to the point, half way underneath me, and I was willing to bet money that Abel was behind me.

"What on earth?" I muttered drowsily. I hadn't remembered falling asleep.

The door creaked and I swear my heart froze inside my chest. Someone had opened my door and was watching us in bed, that's what had woken me up.

I heard the floorboards in the hallway creak as their heavy footsteps took them down the hallway, then down the stairs.

Dash hadn't come home before we'd fallen asleep, it had been Tyson who'd showed up to make sure Abel was okay and once he saw that he was he got the heck out of here. I had no reason to be frightened, it was probably Dash or one of the other guys. No one else would have been able to get into the house without a key and the code to the security box on the wall in the mud room. A security box I was pretty sure that was only there because I lived here now. Something I couldn't bitch about because it made me feel a whole lot safer knowing it was there and that the system was activated.

Still, I needed to get up and check anyways. Just to be safe. I wouldn't be able to fall back asleep until I knew for sure who'd been peeking in the room at us. I wanted to know who'd intruded on our private, intimate moment, which is what I felt us sleeping together was. Not that it would bother me if it was one of the guys because it wouldn't. I was becoming more and more comfortable with intimacy and the fact that there might, more often than not, be more than one of them in the room with me when it happened. I was surprisingly okay with it now.

I carefully untangled my limbs from the twins and crawled down to the bottom of the bed where I climbed off. It was difficult because neither of them wanted to let me go and I had to practically pry their hands off of me.

I stood at the foot of the bed and stared dumbfounded at the two of them in my bed. Addison had rolled over on to his side and flung his arm around his brother's middle. The blanket hung down around their waists. Abel moved easily into his brothers' arms. They held on tightly to each other and I smiled at the sight. They looked sweet together, cute even. I wondered if their physical closeness and the ease with which they shared that physical closeness had anything to do with sharing a womb together for nine months. I imagined it did.

At one point, I had envied them their closeness, their bond. I no longer envied them for it. I was the lucky one because I got to be the one who they put in between them. I no longer had anything to be envious about when it came to them.

Tearing my eyes off of them and walking out my bedroom door was one of the hardest things I'd had to do in my life. Especially when what I really wanted to do was crawl back in bed with them.

I yawned as I peeked into Dash's bedroom. I'd found it empty of the living and not even Binx was around to greet me. That made me feel better. If Binx didn't like the person downstairs then he'd still be up here with the rest of us. He was a snotty little beast and very particular about who he spent his time with.

I walked around the banister and started down the stairs. When I made it to the bottom my eyes scanned through the empty dining room. Nobody there.

I went left in the direction of the kitchen. Nobody there, either. That left the living room. I had really thought to have found whoever in the kitchen. Especially if it was Dash. The kitchen was his favorite room in the house and I often found him in there sitting at the small table, drinking coffee.

Now the room was dark, empty and there wasn't a soul to be seen. Not even a fluffy black cat sitting on the counter to irritate me.

That cat was a serious pain in my behind.

I turned around and moved through the dark dining room heading straight towards the living room. At least the light was on in there so I knew I was headed in the right direction.

I hesitated before turning the corner and walking into the living room because I didn't know what would greet me when I rounded the corner. What or who.

I shouldn't have been surprised by the sight that met me.

Quinton and Dash both seated on the couch with the middle cushion in between them. Their legs were sprawled out in front of them as they slouched down in the couch. I also wasn't surprised to see that it was Quinton who held the remote control aloft in his hand with it aimed at the television. No way would Dash have the remote control with Quinton in the room. They both might have been pure alpha males but only the one could lead the pack. And that was Quinton. Dash was too damaged to be in charge of everything and he didn't seem to ever mind this in the least bit. He gave his opinion, but he did it quietly and efficiently, but he always did it while demanding respect from you. Quinton didn't demand it, either you gave it to him or he didn't have anything to do with you.

I snapped my fingers and they both jumped. The television also turned off.

Alright. I was getting better and better at this magic game by the day.

They turned in the couch to look at me. My shoulder rested against the doorjamb as I watched them, the picture of relaxation when I was anything but.

"Ariel," Quinton said my name slowly.

"You scared us." Dash told me. "I thought you were sleeping."

I had been. Until one of them checked on me.

"What are you doing here, Quint?" I asked.

He'd been the one to check on me. I just knew it. Dash wouldn't have intruded. Not when he knew the twins were here. He was the best roommate a girl could have. He gave me my space when he thought I needed it. He made me coffee and brought it up to me in the morning. He did the laundry and even went so far as to fold my clothes neatly and put them away in my dresser. Even when I asked him not to do these things he went ahead and did them anyways. It used to annoy me but then he told me he actually liked doing these things, it apparently made him feel good. I left him to it after that. I wanted him to be happy and if doing my laundry helped him with that then more power to him. Doing those things didn't bring me joy, they were a chore to me and it actually felt good to have someone taking care of me for the first time in my life. I was used to doing everything for myself.

"Do you not want me here?" Quinton asked and I rolled my

eyes. Of course he wouldn't just straight out answer my question. It always had to be the hard way or no way with him.

"Of course I want you here," I said in exasperation. "What I want to know is why you're here. And why were you checking up on me in my room?"

Quinton's hand went to the back of his neck and he dug his fingers into the skin there. He looked uncomfortable, nervous even. Dash smirked at me and I raised my eyebrows in question.

Watching Quinton squirm was a new thing for me and I had to admit that I kind of liked it. Nobody ever put him in the hot seat. People were too scared of him so he got away with everything. Unless he was dealing with me, of course. I didn't let him get away with anything. Ever. He deserved it, though. For being a bossy prick most of the time, he deserved a lot.

"Quint," I prompted.

"Well..." He mumbled and my lips parted in surprise. What was this? Now he looked even more uncomfortable.

Dash's body shook in silent laughter.

"I'm here to check on the twins, not you," Quinton said in a rush.

"What?" I asked stupidly. "Why are you here to check on them? You live with them. Couldn't you just wait until they came home to check on them? Why do you always have to be so damn pushy? They should be able to have a night without Daddy Quinton telling them what to do and treating them like children."

Okay, so maybe that came out sounding a whole lot harsher than I had anticipated it coming out as. But I really didn't like the way he'd treated Abel earlier. It pissed me off.

Quinton dropped his hand and leaned forward. He placed his elbows on his knees and dropped his head into his hands.

"I fucked up earlier," he muttered through his hands and I stared at him in shock.

What was this? Quinton admitting he'd been wrong. I was shocked. What's more, I didn't take pleasure in his admission. Instead, I felt sorry for him. His job wasn't an easy one and I didn't envy him it. I had enough trouble trying to juggle a few of them at a time and he took on the role of caretaker for all of them. Well, now us.

"I'm going to sleep on the couch here tonight," Quinton muttered. "So that way maybe I can get them to talk to me in the morning."

I studied him with his head held in his hands in a show of defeat and my shoulders slumped. I couldn't be upset with him anymore because of how he looked now.

"I got this," I told him and his head immediately snapped up and he turned to look at me.

"You've got what?"

"The twins," I explained. "I can take care of them and make sure they're okay."

His hands dropped to his knees and he frowned at me. "By take care of them do you mean have sex with them?" He asked me seriously.

Dash stopped laughing silently and burst out with loud laughter. He wrapped his hands around his middle and slumped back into the couch as he roared with laughter.

"You competitive bastard," Dash said through his laughter.

"They won't have sex with me," I blurted. "No one will have sex with me. Not even Ty."

Dash immediately stopped laughing and gaped at me.

"They don't think you're ready," Quinton said quietly.

"The only person who has the answer to that is me," I replied.

"Are you-"

I pushed away from the wall and turned to head back up to my room. Over my shoulder I called, "You can apologize to them tomorrow but let it go at that. I don't need you making things worse because you're a turd."

Dash started laughing again.

Whatever.

"Ariel," Quinton called out my name after me. I didn't stop to talk to him. I went upstairs and left him alone in the living room with Dash. If he wanted to talk about having sex with someone he could do it with Dash for all I cared.

I had every intention of getting back into my own bed and going back to sleep but this plan was thwarted the moment I entered my room. The twins had turned and no longer had their arms wrapped around each other. Instead they were on their sides and back to back. Their knees were cocked out and the bottoms of their feet were pressed together.

I grabbed my cellphone off of my dresser and quickly snapped a picture of them together like that.

I put the phone back on the dresser and laid down on the love seat.

I fell asleep watching girls dressed in expensive clothing be tormented by some undead dead person.

And I did it happy.

This had been the absolute *best* Halloween ever.

THE END.

THANK YOU FOR READING MY BOOK.

The next full-length Ariel Kimber Novel will be coming out some time in 2019. I do not have an exact date at this time and when I do I will post it in my group and on my facebook page. Thank you for reading Good Witch, Bad Witch. If you've enjoyed this short story, please consider leaving a review. Reviews mean the world to us Indie Authors and we appreciate everyone who takes the time to leave one.

Made in the USA
Middletown, DE
30 June 2021